Cinderella CLEANERS

Scheme Spirit

Read all the Cinderella Cleaners books!

Scheme Spirit

MAYA GOLD

SCHOLASTIC INC.

New York   Toronto   London   Auckland
Sydney   Mexico City   New Delhi   Hong Kong

ISBN 978-0-545-22768-1

12 11 10 9 8 7 6 5 4 3 2 1   10 11 12 13 14 15/0

Printed in the U.S.A.   40
First edition, November 2010

Book design by Yaffa Jaskoll

To Papa and Nani,
with love and thanks

Chapter One

I wish there was a law against having math class last period. The only numbers I can possibly concentrate on at this time of day are the ones on the clock, as the second hand ticks oh-so-slowly toward freedom.

It doesn't help that my teacher, Mr. Perotta, is standing directly in front of the Homecoming parade poster that's tacked up on the bulletin board. Most schools have Homecoming in October, but Weehawken, New Jersey, where I've lived all my life, is right across the Hudson River from a *very* famous parade. In fact, the giant balloons for the Macy's Thanksgiving Day Parade are stored in an old Pepsi warehouse here and get trucked into New York through the Lincoln Tunnel, a few blocks away. So our town's tradition is to throw our own big parade on the weekend before Thanksgiving. This year's poster has a turkey design, and Mr. Perotta is standing so close that it looks like the drumstick is coming right out of his ear.

My best friend, Jess Munson, is sitting diagonally in front of me. I wonder if she's noticed our teacher's new look. I try to catch her eye, but she's bending forward, her springy red curls nearly hiding her face as her pencil moves eagerly over her loose-leaf notebook. If you didn't know any better, you'd assume she was taking notes as Mr. Perotta drones on about dodecahedrons, but I'm sitting at just the right angle to see that she's doodling flowers and cartoon monsters all over the margin.

I can't help smiling, since my own notebook's margins are totally covered with fashion sketches. Still, I don't want Mr. Perotta to ask, "What's so funny?" or worse yet, to come see for himself, so I turn my head. But the view to my left is way more distracting than Jess's doodles or the Homecoming poster. The second-floor windows look across the river at the world's most spectacular skyline. The sun's glinting off the chrome spires of the Chrysler Building and the Empire State Building, and I picture a giant silk banner flapping between them, with the words:

DIANA DONATO, WISH YOU WERE HERE!

No such luck. I'm in eighth-grade math, and as soon as the bell rings, I'll be heading to work at my family's dry-cleaning business, Cinderella Cleaners. I've been helping out there ever since my stepmother, Fay, decided I was old enough to work after school instead of being in the Drama Club's fall play, *Our Town*. I was pretty mad about having to work there at first, but the cleaners turned out to be way more fun than I could have ever imagined. I've made some great friends, learned a little about tailoring and design, and had some amazing adventures. So no regrets, right?

Well, maybe one. This afternoon our Drama Club advisor, Ms. Wyant, is posting the sign-up sheet for the holiday show, *The Snow Queen*. It was bad enough missing out on *Our Town*, my favorite play in the world, but *The Snow Queen* is a *musical*.

If there's anything I love more than getting to act, it's getting to sing, dance, *and* act. All I want to do when the bell rings in (count 'em) twelve seconds is beat a path to Ms. Wyant's door to sign up for auditions. Which is exactly what Jess will be doing without me. I wouldn't say that I'm jealous, but . . .

Three . . . two . . . one . . . *BRRRRRRINNNG!*

The classroom erupts in a sudden stampede. Jess slams her notebook shut and jumps up, turning toward me.

"Come on!" she says breathlessly. "Help me sign up!"

Help her sign up? I don't really get why she'd need help, and I don't have a whole lot of turnaround time before I need to be on the bus to the cleaners. Plus it's bound to make me feel even more I'm-not-saying-jealous to go to Ms. Wyant's classroom and *not* put my name on the sign-up sheet.

But Jess is my best friend, and I wouldn't dream of leaving her hanging.

"You bet," I say, scooping my own notebook into my backpack and waving good-bye to our friends Sara Parvati and Amelia Williams. Math is the only class all four of us have together, and we fall into neat pairs: Sara's a straight-A math whiz and Amelia loves number puzzles like sudoku and kenken. They're also both soccer fanatics, while Jess and I live and breathe theatre, music, and art. We used to call ourselves the Left Brain/Right Brain Club.

So today the left brainiacs are heading to soccer practice, and we right-brained creatives are going to Drama Club, one to sign up and one just passing through.

"I'm *so* excited!" says Jess as she grabs my hand, pulling me through the after-school swarm in the hall. She's perfected the art of rushing just enough to get where she's going without having teachers call after her, "No running in the halls!"

Even so, we're not the first to arrive at Ms. Wyant's door. That would be Riley Jackson, a lanky African-American boy in our class with a really sensational voice. He played Henry Higgins and I played Eliza Doolittle when the Drama Club did *My Fair Lady* last year. Riley's writing his name on the top of the list with a bright orange Sharpie. His signature looks like an autograph.

"Can't miss *that*," says Jess, bending to write her own name right under his.

"That's the point," Riley grins as he snaps the cap back on his Sharpie. "Hey, Diana, are you trying out for this one?" His tone is hopeful, which makes me happy and sad at the same time.

5

I shake my head. "I've got work every day after school. I can't go to rehearsals."

"Hello, young stars," says Ms. Wyant, coming out of her classroom with her trademark big smile. She once told us that when she was fresh out of college and at her first-ever screen test, the casting director said, "You'll never work in commercials with *that* set of gums." But I think she's gorgeous. And she's taught us so much about acting, auditions, and *life*.

"About those rehearsals, Diana," Ms. Wyant says, clearly having caught the tail end of our conversation. "Do you think your father might be willing to let you miss work for just one week? It would be the last five days of rehearsals before the show."

"I'm not sure," I say honestly, but my heart starts beating faster.

"If so, there might be a role you could do," Ms. Wyant explains. "It's a solo."

A *solo*! My heartbeat speeds up.

"You mean the Enchantress?" says Riley, and Ms. Wyant nods.

"Of course!" cries Jess. "You'd be *perfect*, Diana!"

I haven't read the script — I thought it would just make me feel even worse. But as soon as I hear "the Enchantress" my imagination goes into overdrive. As Ms. Wyant explains that the character sings a song that casts a spell, plunging the kingdom into a winter that lasts for ten years, I picture myself in the silvery robes and fur-trimmed cloak of Narnia's evil White Witch. It gives me the shivers. In a good way.

"I'm planning to stage the Enchantress's song in front of the curtain while the stage crew is changing the set to a snow scene behind," she explains. "So there's no one else in the scene. If you get the part, we could work on the music together during your study hall, or at lunch. You'd just have to commit to come in every day during tech week."

"That would be amazing," I tell her, feeling as if the clouds have just parted to let in a ray of bright sunshine. "I'll ask my dad this afternoon."

"Auditions are tomorrow and Thursday," she smiles, tapping the sign-up sheet. "Bring a prepared song — anything you'd like to sing — and I'll let you go first, so you won't miss your bus."

"Thank you so much!" I can feel my eyes shining. What am I going to sing? My mind's turning cartwheels.

Not so fast, I remind myself. Dad hasn't given permission yet, and there's no guarantee that he will. I take a deep breath, trying to hold down my skyrocketing hopes, though it's probably already too late. Once I start dreaming about something I want, it's hard to let go of it. I'm stubborn that way.

"Here," says Ms. Wyant, and hands me a script; Jess and Riley already have theirs from earlier Drama Club meetings. I clutch mine against my chest like a good luck charm as Jess and I rush toward our lockers. But as soon as we turn the corner, we run smack into my least favorite person in Drama Club, Kayleigh Carell. As always, she's with her matching blond sidekick, Savannah Bates. They're both dressed in full cheerleader outfits. They haven't had time to change clothes since the bell rang, so they must have been wearing their uniforms all afternoon, just so the rest of us know they've got cheerleading practice today.

What is it about being a cheerleader that makes everyone think you're the queen of the universe? What's the big deal about wearing a short skirt and learning a few simple arm movements? News flash: *Anybody* can jump in the air and yell, "Tick, tick, boom!"

Not that I'd ever want to. But surely I *could*.

All the middle school cheerleaders strut down the halls as if they own the school, and they're all *obsessed* with making it into the big league: the varsity cheer squad at Weehawken High. But Kayleigh's the worst, because not only does she give off cheerleader attitude 24/7; she also thinks she's the star of the Drama Club.

Now, *that's* getting personal. Jess and I have been acting since we were in preschool, where we played both ends of the Cow That Jumped Over the Moon. I was the head and front legs, and Jess was the tail end that got all the laughs. With her wild red curls and great sense of timing, Jess still prefers playing comic parts. Which leaves me and Kayleigh duking it out for the leads.

"What are you doing with *that*?" Kayleigh demands, pointing a polished pink fingernail at my script for *The Snow Queen*.

"She's going to try out," says Jess. "So am I."

Kayleigh shoots Jess a you're-not-even-worth-answering glare and turns toward me, tossing her ponytail over one shoulder. "Don't you have to work at the laundromat?"

"It's a dry cleaner," I say. I can feel my ears burning. "And yes, I do have to work there. But Ms. Wyant's letting me audition anyway."

"Must be because she's so *good*," Jess says loyally.

Savannah lets out a little snort, like a whinnying pony. "Yeah, right," she says. I notice she's carrying two sets of pom-poms: her own and Kayleigh's. Imagine if Jess made me carry her Mad Hatter top hat around, like a lady-in-waiting.

"You know what, Diana?" says Kayleigh, her voice going syrupy. "I'm glad you're going to try out. It'll be nice to have *some* competition."

If only. Even if Dad lets me try out, the lead is off-limits — I'd have to be free to rehearse every day. Jess has her eye on the role of Court Jester, and most of the other girls who can sing well are sixth and seventh graders, so unless Ms. Wyant casts a newbie, Kayleigh will probably be wearing the Snow Queen's tiara.

Just what we need from her: more royal attitude.

As if she were reading my thoughts, Kayleigh scans my outfit from top to toe. My brown hair is pulled back with a small rhinestone clip, and I'm wearing a vintage angora cardigan over a pastel pink cami, black skirt, and tights, plus my signature Converse high-tops with two different laces (neon yellow and pink this week).

"Where did you pick up that sweater, the Salvation Army?" she smirks.

Actually, it was Goodwill, but I don't expect country-club Kayleigh to get how much fun it is trolling through racks of secondhand clothes for the odd buried treasure. For her, "used" means you've worn it to school more than once.

But I don't have enough nerve to confront her head-on. The only time I've ever stood up to Kayleigh was when I was wearing a mask and she thought I was somebody else, a rich girl named Taylor with famous friends. It felt pretty sweet, but "Taylor" did not have to face Kayleigh's snap judgments day in and day out, like I do when I'm just plain Diana. And ever since that masquerade ball, when Kayleigh's boyfriend, Ethan Horowitz, broke up with her and went trick-or-treating with our group of friends

11

instead, she's been even snootier toward Jess and me than usual.

I'm trying to figure out how to snap back at that crack about my vintage sweater — something sharp enough to make me feel I'm not being a doormat, but not such a burn it'll make Kayleigh pick on me more — when Ms. Wyant comes around the corner. She's holding an empty coffee mug and is clearly on her way to the teachers' lounge.

"Hello, young stars!" she says again. It's her usual greeting, but the effect on Kayleigh is instantaneous. In a blink, she's transformed from a sneering queen bee to a simpering fan. Maybe she *can* act a little.

"Oh, Ms. Wyant," she gushes. "I just love *The Snow Queen*. I was reading the script out loud last night and it made me cry every time."

"Well, good," says Ms. Wyant. "The trick will be making the *audience* cry." She looks at Savannah. "Are you trying out?"

Savannah shakes her head, giggling. "I'm shy."

She's about as shy as a squawking parrot, but fine.

"We can always use help on the stage crew, Savannah," Ms. Wyant says with a smile. "And Kayleigh, be sure to sign up for auditions with Jess and Diana."

"Did you see Kayleigh's face?" Jess gloats as we walk toward my bus. "She looked like she was sucking on lemons."

"Must be 'cause she misses me so," says a boy's voice right behind her. I turn and see Ethan, grinning from ear to ear.

My heart skips a beat when I see that he's with his best friend and my friend-maybe-boyfriend, Will Carson. It's hard to know what to call Will, now that we've taken the plunge and *held hands*. (All right, only once, but still.) There's got to be some better way to describe our relationship, but I don't have a clue what it is. Neither does anyone else, it seems. The English language could really use some new words for those wobbly steps between "just friends" and "couple."

Will's dark hair is in its usual bed-head tumble, and he's wearing a new entry from his seemingly bottomless drawer of T-shirts with band logos. This time it's the Kings of Leon, a funny design with a fake necktie stenciled below the neck. It looks really cute peeking from his jean jacket.

I smile, glad to see Will as always, and he smiles back awkwardly. Now, if *he* told Ms. Wyant that he was shy, he'd be telling the truth. He might work on the sound crew, but there's no way he'd ever perform on a stage. The only exception is when he's holding one of his instruments: either the bass guitar he plays with his big brother's mad cool rock band, or the euphonium, the tuba-like horn he plays in the middle school stage band. You get to see the real Will when he's doing his music. Just like you see the real me when I'm acting.

Neither Jess nor Ethan has such a problem. What you see is what you get. They tease each other nonstop, but sometimes I think it's because they're so much alike. I wonder if Ethan, with his blue eyes, cleft in his chin, and oversize ego, thinks Jess has a crush on him. But she totally doesn't; Jess is dating a super-cute boy from a nearby prep school. Still, Ethan seems to get a kick out of any attention paid to him, even negative attention. Like now, when Jess swats his arm with her Mad Hatter top hat.

"Dream on," she says. "Who would miss *you*?"

"Anybody with taste," Ethan shrugs. "Though I guess that excludes any girl who wears top hats."

"That's just what your cheerleader girlfriend thinks," Jess responds.

"*Ex*-girlfriend. Accent on *ex*," Ethan says. "Not a moment too soon either. Kayleigh's parents are throwing a luau theme party Saturday night, right after the Homecoming game. They'd probably want me to dress as a pineapple."

Since Kayleigh's parents made Ethan wear a red-and-gold clown suit to the masquerade ball, that's probably not far from the truth.

"But you guys are both going on Saturday, right?" I ask, looking at Will.

"What, to the luau? No way!" Ethan says with a shudder. "One ukulele and I would be toast."

"I meant to Homecoming," I say.

I love our town's Homecoming tradition. There's always

a big parade with fire trucks, banners, and floats sponsored by local groups or decorated in the high school's colors, blue and white. The high school marching band struts its stuff, and the local police have a bagpipe and drum corps. There's a cool ceremony where the senior class officers crown the Homecoming king, queen, and court right before the big game, and the whole crowd does the Wave. And even though I'm not as much of a football fan as Amelia and Sara, there's something incredibly exciting about sitting in the bleachers with your friends and roaring, "Go, team!"

Even though there are bound to be cheerleaders.

This year, Homecoming should be even more fun than usual. Jess, Amelia, Sara, and I have always gone with somebody's parents — usually Amelia's dad, who played football in high school — but this year we've gotten permission to sit by ourselves for the first time ever. I'm hoping Will and Ethan will join us, too.

"I'll be in the parade," says Will. "Playing euphonium."

"Really?" I say, surprised. "I thought only the high school band marches."

Will shrugs. "I'm in it. They're short on euphoniums."

"I believe it," says Ethan. "Who'd play an instrument you can't pronounce?"

"*You* can't pronounce *guitar*," Jess says. "So you don't count."

"That is so cool!" I tell Will. I'm really impressed. That is just like him, to be in the high school band when he's still in eighth grade and not even mention it. "We'll be at the parade with Amelia and Sara."

"And Jason," says Jess with a really bright smile.

"Oh, *Jaaaa-son*," says Ethan in an exaggerated posh accent that sounds like *Project Runway*'s Tim Gunn. "So the preppy prince stoops to attend an event with us public school bottom-feeders?"

"Who said anything about going with *you*?" Jess responds, grinning. They might keep this up for the rest of the afternoon, but the school buses let off their warning horn blast.

"Bye, guys!" I say, running off as they all chorus, "Bye!" Is it my imagination, or is Will's smile the widest?

Chapter Two

I keep my face pressed to the window as the bus pulls out of the driveway and heads down Underhill Avenue. Now that it's November and most of the trees are bare, the view of the river is even more striking. Today the water's slate gray, with a big red barge sewing a seam down the middle. There's my buddy the Empire State Building, standing head and shoulders above the other skyscrapers. Someday I'll live in one of those high-rise buildings and take yellow taxis to work in a Broadway show. I'll walk in through the stage door, say hello to the costume assistant, and head for my dressing room. It will be heaven.

Meanwhile, at least I can dream about getting cast in *The Snow Queen*. What am I going to sing for auditions?

And what am I going to *wear*? I love these decisions!

I pull out the script and flip through the pages till I find the Enchantress's song. Maybe something in the lyrics will suggest the right outfit. Not for the first time, I wish I could sight-read sheet music, so I could sound out the melody. Mom wanted me to take piano lessons like she did when she was a girl, but that was just one of the things that got put on hold when we found out she had cancer.

Don't think about that now, I tell myself firmly. Sometimes I wonder if it's ever going to stop hurting. But I'm getting better at chasing bad memories away by picturing something else that makes me happy. So I imagine that Mom's looking over my shoulder as I read the lyrics to the Enchantress's song.

Songs are a little like poems, and even without any music, the words to this one, about snowflakes falling and falling, the world spinning white, are hypnotic. It's been such a long time since I got to sing. I remember how I felt as I twirled around in my ball gown from *My Fair Lady*, singing "I Could Have Danced All Night," and feel a weight lift off my shoulders. Dad *has* to let me try out for *The Snow Queen*!

Actually, Dad might be the least of my worries. Though he's been running Cinderella Cleaners since my grandpapa retired a few years ago, it was my stepmother, Fay, who insisted that I should start working there after school. It's partly to save on expenses, and partly because Fay thinks it's good for my character.

The jury is still out on that one. The job has made me a hard worker, and it's taught me to be more organized about homework (well, most of the time), but it's also offered some temptations I couldn't resist. I'm surrounded by clothes every day, and the actress in me wants to try them all on. Sometimes I actually do, and wind up on adventures that may not be what Fay had in mind for improving my character . . . though I wouldn't have missed them for anything.

But I've promised Dad I'll turn over a new leaf at work, and ever since Halloween, when I made a costume piece out of a customer's tablecloth, by mistake, I've been a perfect employee. I'm no longer allowed to take clothes from our in-house thrift store, the No Pickup rack, where garments that aren't claimed by customers sit for a month before being given away to employees or charity. (The tablecloth hadn't been on it the full thirty days — I forgot to check.) And my friend Cat and I have stopped sneaking into the cold-storage fur vault to try on coats during our afternoon break.

Though who knows, there might be a white fox fur cape in there that would be *perfect* for the Enchantress!

That's enough of that, I tell myself sternly, and turn my thoughts to Saturday's Homecoming parade again. I'm trying to picture shy Will in one of the high school marching band's blue-and-white uniforms, with their military rows of brass buttons and tall feathered hats. I bet he'll feel really geeky and look really cute. I feel myself blush, and I hope that Jess, Amelia, and Sara won't start teasing me about Will during the parade. I'll blush even more then!

My friends are all planning to meet at our usual spot, right in front of the Jolly Cow ice cream stand. It closes each year on Thanksgiving, so it's always our last chocolate dip twist cone with rainbow sprinkles till Easter. It's tradition. And what could be better than eating ice cream with your best friends while you watch a parade? Just thinking about it makes me feel like waving a flag. I can't wait!

The bus is only a few blocks away from Cinderella Cleaners, and I can see its rooftop pink neon crown looming over the gas stations and strip malls. When we reach the gleaming chrome of Sam's Diner, it's time for me to get off.

The wind nips my cheeks as I scurry across the parking lot and circle around back to what I can't resist calling the stage door, even though it says EMPLOYEE ENTRANCE in capital letters. I've got the routine down by now, and I stamp my time card, pick up my smock, and enter the dressing room like an old pro. After stashing my backpack and coat in my locker, I open the door to the workroom, bracing myself for the blast of warm air, machine sounds, and radio music. Everybody greets me with a wave or a smile as I pass, circling around sorting tables and bins full of clothes on my way to the front. I feel right at home.

Once I pass through the swinging doors into Customer Service, the atmosphere is distinctly cooler, and not just because I've left the hot dryer vents and steam presses behind. There are only two people at Cinderella Cleaners who don't like me, and they're standing side by side at the counter.

My supervisor, Miss MacInerny, is at the cash register, totaling an order. She's been working here since Dad was my age, so she's probably earned her crabbiness rights (not to mention her nickname of Joyless). But the young woman next to her, Lara Nekrasova, is a total mystery. Lara was just promoted from the back room to Customer Service, and she seems to have sprouted a new personality to match her new job. If it weren't for her pretty, high-cheekboned face and musical Russian accent, I'd say she was Joyless's clone.

Neither one of them greets me, which is a definite improvement over the usual "You're late" or "What took you so long?" Joyless is counting out change, and Lara is working the conveyor belt's foot pedal, keeping her eye on the clothes swishing past in their clear plastic bags until she spots her customer's order. So I walk right past them, flip up the hinged counter section, and go to Dad's office.

His door's open, as it usually is unless he's going over books with his accountant. I walk right in, and as always, his whole face lights up when he sees me. He gets up from his desk chair and gives me a hug, pulling my cheek against his freshly pressed shirt. My whole family smells like clean laundry.

"How was school?" he asks.

"Fine." And I hesitate. I really want to ask whether I can try out for *The Snow Queen*, but I'm still on probation for making a mermaid tail out of that tablecloth. What if Dad thinks I'm not committed enough to keep on working here? A couple of months ago, I would have leapt at the chance to quit my after-school job and go back to drama full-time, but I've fallen in love with the cleaners. The truth is, I'd miss it like crazy if I had to leave.

"Okay, what is it?" Dad asks, studying me.

This is the thing about being an only child. Dad's always been able to read my moods. And after Mom died, when it was just the two of us living together, too shellshocked to use many words, it was almost like we were both psychic. That didn't change when my grandparents moved in to help Dad take care of me. People used to call us two peas in a pod.

Our pod changed a lot when Fay and her twin daughters, Ashley and Brynna, came into the picture. After Dad got remarried, Papa and Nonni not only moved out of our house to make room for them, they retired to Miami Beach. I miss them a lot. Papa's silly postcards of manatees and sand dollars make me smile, but not the way he does.

"Diana?" Dad asks in a prompting tone.

I could tell him about our new social studies assignment to research local place names, or say something bland about weather, but he'd see right through it. Besides, it's a chance to be part of the holiday show! So I tell him what Ms. Wyant offered.

"It's a *solo*," I say, my voice lifting with breathless excitement.

"And when is the show?"

"The weekend before Christmas vacation."

Dad looks me over, considering it. "The holiday season's our busiest time," he says. "From Thanksgiving to Christmas, it all just explodes. Winter coats, party clothes, seasonal businesses . . . And I'm sure you remember that you need to pay for replacing that tablecloth."

I nod, disappointed. Why did I think he'd say yes?

But Dad isn't done yet. "I'll tell you what, though. I could use some more hands on these next busy weekends. You said that Ms. Wyant will need you for five days during — what is it called again, tech week? So let's make a trade. I'll give you those five afternoons off if you'll come in to work for the next five Saturdays."

"Dad, that's fantastic!" I say, moving to hug him. And then I remember. The Homecoming parade!

"Something wrong?" he says, reading my change of expression.

"Not exactly . . . It's just that this Saturday's Homecoming, and I've already made plans to go with my friends."

Dad raises his eyebrows. I'm afraid he's going to tell me that I'm trying to have my cake and eat it too, or look a gift horse in the mouth, or one of those other parent clichés. But he just says mildly, "Well, then, you've got a decision to make. Which is more important to you?"

The holiday show or Homecoming? How can I choose between two things I love?

Again, Dad sees me hesitate. "You don't have to tell me today," he says. "Just think it over."

So that's what I do. As I'm rolling clothes bins from the customer counter to the sorting table, or putting white cardboard bands inside the collars of freshly pressed button-down shirts, I try to picture myself in each place. There I am in my white fox fur cloak, in a pool of bright spotlight in front of the black velvet curtain. I'm singing my heart out and I'm full of joy.

And right over there is another me, equally joyous, dressed up in school-spirit blue and white clothes with a cluster of friends. I'm licking rainbow sprinkles off Jolly Cow cones while we're waiting for Will to march by with the band. And just like that, I get it. They're both happy pictures, but one is performing onstage and the other is being a part of the audience.

I have to go with the holiday show.

At least that's what I think until Cat rushes in, pulling her light green smock over a T-shirt the color of mango sorbet. She has to drive all the way down from the high school, so she's always running a few minutes late.

"The traffic was crazy," she says, pulling her thick black hair into a ponytail and joining me next to the bagging machine. "How come every Toyota in town has to cruise past the Underhill Deli at just the same time? It was bumper to bumper. I felt like a New York City cabdriver."

"Well, you made it," I tell her.

"Yeah, eight minutes late. Hey, you got all those shirt collars finished already? Good woman." Cat picks up the shirts and starts bagging them expertly.

"Catalina?" I ask, using her full name to get her attention. "What if you had to decide between two things you totally love? How would you make up your mind?"

"Give me some specifics," says Cat.

"Okay, singing a solo onstage, or going to Homecoming with my besties."

"No-brainer," says Cat automatically. "Homecoming."

Now I'm sorry I asked her. "Really? For sure?"

"I *love* Homecoming," says Cat. "It's my favorite thing about living in Weehawken. And I'm totally bummed that I'll have to miss it this year."

"What are you doing on Saturday?" I ask, hoping I'm not being nosy.

"Working right here, *chica*. Saving up cash for my beautiful car."

That's right — I'd forgotten that Cat started working here on Saturdays when she made the down payment on a used car. If I do make the trade Dad offered me, I'd be working with her every Saturday. That is a definite plus.

Cat is still talking. "My best friend, Marina, she's on student council with me, and she's gonna be crowning the Homecoming court this year. It's a really big honor. She's totally stoked. And I'm gonna miss the whole thing paying for my PT Cruiser."

"Can't you take a personal day?"

Cat shakes her head. "I need the bucks. Jared gave me a great birthday present — these earrings, see, aren't they the bomb? — and *his* birthday is right after Thanksgiving. Between him and my Cruiser, I can't take off work."

I'm still not used to having a friend who's old enough to be buying a car, not to mention getting an expensive gift for her *boyfriend*. Cat is a junior in high school, but sometimes the three and a half years between us feels enormous. It's hard to imagine I'll ever be quite that grown-up. Then I remember my nine-and-a-half-year-old stepsisters, and feel like I already am.

"Seriously, don't even think about missing Homecoming," Cat says. "It totally rocks."

I shake my head. "I already decided. If I get cast in the show, I'm working here Saturdays."

"Fine," says Cat sarcastically, raising her eyebrows. "I'm *so* glad you asked my advice." She flashes a grin to show me she's kidding, then hangs up the row of bagged button-down shirts as I roll an empty cart back to the customer counter.

Dad is seeing an elderly customer, Mrs. Litzky, out to her car. I watch through the window as he hangs her dry cleaning in the backseat. With a pang, I realize that our front window features a Homecoming poster.

How am I going to tell Amelia and Sara I'm not going to join them? Jess would make the same choice herself, so she'll get it, but my sporty friends won't understand. Amelia would not miss a game for *anything* — especially not for a musical.

Well, they'll just have to accept my decision. My mind is made up.

I watch Dad wave good-bye to Mrs. Litzky and head back inside. Before I can waver, I walk over and tell him, "I made a decision. If Ms. Wyant gives me the part, I'll work all five Saturdays."

He looks at me. "Are you totally sure?"

I nod. "I really want to be in *The Snow Queen*. If I have to miss Homecoming this year, I will. It's worth it."

"I'm glad," says Dad. "It'll do my heart good to hear you sing a solo." He kisses the top of my head, and as we move apart, I see Lara staring at me with a narrow-eyed frown. What has she got against me? Are she and Kayleigh Carell in some kind of a We Hate Diana Club?

Whatever it is, I'm getting sick of it. As Dad goes back into his office, I walk up to the counter and look Lara right in the eye. "Can I ask you something?"

Lara shrugs. "Vat is it?"

"Were you ever a cheerleader?"

If Lara's surprised by my question, she doesn't blink.

"In high school, yes. First year that my family is livink here, I try out for team. Senior year I vas captain."

Does that figure, or what? I smile to myself as I push through the double doors into the workroom. The cleaning machines are all tumbling at once, making so much noise that no one will notice or care if I sing every song I've ever learned as I work. I've got an audition to prep.

Chapter Three

By the time Jess makes her nightly phone call, I've narrowed it down to three favorite songs — I think. I've got sheet music littered all over my bed, so my homework is practically buried. (I did get it finished, though — part of my promise to Dad.)

"So what song did you pick?" Jess asks right away. I've already texted her that Dad said yes, and her reply was a screen full of exclamation marks.

"Definitely a ballad, but I can't decide between *Phantom*, *Rent*, and *Angel*."

"*Angel*," says Jess without missing a beat.

It's our new favorite show, especially since I went to opening night and got to meet the stars. I've been singing along to my autographed CD of the sound track ever since.

"You think?" I ask.

"Duh. It's *perfect* for you. Plus it's new, so nobody else will be doing it."

"Nobody blond, you mean."

"Bingo," says Jess. Then she sings me the audition song she's picked out, from one of our favorite old musicals, *Guys and Dolls*. It's a hilarious number called "Adelaide's Lament," and she really belts it out — not always in tune, but she nails every laugh.

"What do you think?" she asks breathlessly.

"That was sick!" I say, still cracking up. "I love how you sang 'la post-nasal drip.' You really sounded like you have a cold."

"I do," says Jess. "That's why I picked that song."

"Good choice," I say, grinning. I pick up the sheet music from *Angel*, but before I can sing the first note, there's a rap on my door.

"You've been on the phone long enough," Fay calls from the hallway. "It's bedtime."

It's a good thing the door is still shut so she can't see me rolling my eyes. "All right," I call out to her — and reluctantly say good-bye to Jess.

All day long on Thursday, my stomach feels like a whole flock of butterflies is having a dance party. Ms. Wyant is giving me an extra-early audition slot, even before the group warm-up, so I won't be late for work. It's really nice of her, but it means I'll be up onstage singing while everyone's still coming in, and I'm totally nervous.

The second the bell rings, Jess and I rush to our lockers, grabbing our coats, hats, and sheet music, and make a bee-line to the auditorium. On the way, we pass Will, who turns to call after me, "Break a Lorax!" Jess and I have a long, silly tradition of variations on that classic actors' good-luck wish of "break a leg," and I'm sort of touched that he remembered our joke.

"Thanks!" I yell over my shoulder as Jess and I barrel downstairs.

Ms. Wyant is already in the auditorium, checking a clipboard with the stage manager, Gracie Chen. The chorus teacher, Miss Bowman, is doing warm-ups on the piano. She has a short, starchy hairdo that looks more bright yellow than blond, like she dyed it with paint by mistake.

Ms. Wyant looks up and gives me an encouraging smile. "Are you ready?" she asks, and I nod.

The butterfly hoedown goes ballistic as I hand Miss Bowman my sheet music. I can feel my heartbeat in the back of my throat, which is suddenly drier than dry, though I just took a big swig of water. As I walk up the three steps to the stage, I remind myself what Ms. Wyant taught us: An audition begins before you say a word, with the clothes you picked out and the confident way you walk onto the stage. I'm not wearing a costume, of course, but I've chosen a blouse whose wide sleeves remind me of Angel's lacy white dressing gown and replaced my flat Converse with low-heeled boots that make me feel tall and a little more regal, like someone who might get to play an enchantress.

Okay, here I am, center stage. Again, I remember what Ms. Wyant taught us: *Take a moment to claim your position and ground yourself, then make eye contact with the director. Tell her your name and the name of the piece you've prepared as clearly as if they were lines from a play.*

"Hi, I'm Diana Donato," I say with my sawdusty throat. "And I'm singing 'My Outlaw' from *Angel*."

I nod to Miss Bowman, taking a deep breath from the bottom of my lungs as the piano plays the familiar chords of the intro. I open my mouth to sing, and the first few notes come out small and strained. But then somehow the miracle happens. I'm no longer nervous Diana; I'm a Wild West girl named Angel who's fallen in love with a man on the run from the law. Since that character's played in the show by my major celebrity crush, Adam Kessler, whose gorgeous blue eyes I have actually gotten to stare into at close range, it's easy to feel exactly what Angel is feeling.

The glorious high note at the end is a bit of a stretch, and I can feel my voice thinning a little. But when I think of Adam smiling at me, my heart fills with joy and the note seems to soar without effort.

I'm very surprised to hear scattered applause. I got so lost in the song that I barely noticed the rest of the Drama Club entering the auditorium.

Ms. Wyant spins around with a frown. "No applause at auditions. Let's keep this professional, people." She turns back to me. "Thank you, Diana. Cast list will be posted on Friday."

I nod and walk back down the steps, feeling my usual eighth-grade self seeping back to the surface. I better be sure not to trip on my boot heels. That would be classic.

Jess mouths a silent "bravo" as I scoop up my backpack, and I whisper, "Break a lemming!" Riley, who's sitting behind her with Ethan, gives me a quick knuckle bump as I head up the aisle.

"That was awesome," he whispers, and I whisper back, "Thanks!" I'm a little sweaty and flustered but not nervous anymore.

I'm most of the way to the door when I realize I left my sheet music on Miss Bowman's piano. I turn, wondering if I should go back to get it, but Ms. Wyant's already signaling everyone else to come down front for warm-ups. I've got to get to the bus, and besides, Kayleigh's bound to sweep in any second.

Why am I not surprised that she'd time her entrance to miss my audition?

I turn back to the door, and sure enough, there's Kayleigh, dressed in head-to-toe Hollister. She's striking a pose in the doorway as if she were being interviewed on the red carpet. I can't leave the room without walking right past her, but I have no choice: If I miss the bus to the cleaners, I'll be in big trouble.

"Leaving already, Diana?" Kayleigh says with an over-size smile. "What a shame. You're *such* a hard worker."

Well, you know what? I am. So I do the last thing that Kayleigh expects: treat her snarky sarcasm as if she's completely sincere.

"Thank you, Kayleigh," I say. "That's so nice." And I'm out the door before she can figure out if I'm kidding or not, making it onto the bus with just seconds to spare.

Dad was right about one thing — the holiday season *is* busy. Thanksgiving is still eight days away, but the volume of clothes is already much higher than usual. My arms ache from picking up heavy wool blankets and winter coats.

"Look at it this way," says Cat as she flexes a bicep. "It's making us buff."

"Soon you'll be arm wrestling Jared," I tease her. Cat's boyfriend is on the varsity wrestling squad. He's not too

39

much taller than Cat, who stands five feet two wearing heels, but his arms are all muscle.

"That is so not going to happen," says Cat. "Is it time for our break yet?"

I look at the wall clock. "Five minutes. I better go grab one more load." I roll the empty cart through the big double doors, and there in the customer section stands somebody I'm always happy to see: the head tailor, Nelson Martinez. He's wearing one of his typical hipster outfits: a slate gray vest over a white T-shirt paired with black jeans. But on his head is a fuzzy red Santa hat with a white pom-pom. Miss MacInerny is scowling at him, of course, but Nelson's not intimidated by her or anyone else.

"Good look," I grin. "Is that Juicy Couture?"

"Ho, ho, ho," Nelson deadpans as I scan the counter. It's covered with red and white garments.

"Are those *all* Santa suits?" I gasp.

"Give or take the odd elf," Nelson says. " 'Tis the season, for sure. If you find anything that needs mending, bring it over to my North Pole workshop." He shakes his pom-pom at me and strolls to the Tailoring section, ignoring the twin glares of Lara and Joyless.

• • •

Cat can't believe her eyes when I roll in a cart overflowing with Santa suits. "Where did all those come from, the Salvation Army?" she asks.

I shake my head. "Costume rental shop in Passaic. Looks like they're outfitting every mall Santa in northern New Jersey."

Cat picks up a red granny dress with peppermint-striped trim and a little white apron. "This must be Mrs. Claus."

"All you need is the glasses and wig," I say, reaching into the cart. "And look, here's her favorite elf." The elf suit I pull out is bright green and red, with a wide floppy collar. It's paired with a jester hat and oversize curly-toed slippers.

"I dare you," says Cat.

I'm tempted, but I shake my head firmly. "I'm not borrowing clothes anymore. I promised my father."

"Who said anything about borrowing? Just a quick fur-vault fashion show during our break." Cat grins and holds up the Mrs. Claus outfit. "I will if you will."

I look at the clock. It *is* time for our break, and

everybody is too busy working to notice us smuggling a couple of costumes into the fur storage vault.

"Come on," says Cat, reading my thoughts. "Who's gonna know?"

The fur vault is almost as cold as a walk-in fridge, and the most private spot at the cleaners. In the hot days of early fall, Cat and I used to love sneaking in here with our friend Elise — I cracked them both up by trying on fur coats and doing impressions of the people I thought might own them. I can't wait to act out the part of a two-tone elf.

Cat and I barrel in, already giggling, and pull on our costumes right over our clothes. As soon as we see each other, we start cracking up. My elf jacket has a rip under one arm, and I make a mental note that I should flag it for Tailoring as soon as we're finished with our private fashion show. I'm leaning against a silky chinchilla jacket, trying to pull on a curly-toed bootie, when I hear the vault's door swing open. I look up and freeze.

Lara stands on the threshold, holding a customer's pick-up receipt. She doesn't look as surprised as most people would if they opened a storage unit and came across two people dressed as an elf and Mrs. Claus. In fact, I would have to say she looks delighted, the way a cat looks when it's cornered a mouse.

"So this is now dressink room," she says. "Very interestink."

"We were just fooling around," I say quickly, ears flaming.

Cat adds, "We're on break."

Lara does not say a word. She steps into the fur vault and surveys the coats on the left-hand wall, scanning their tag numbers. After a moment she finds one that matches the yellow receipt in her hand, and lifts up a full-length mink coat in a storage bag. Then she heads back toward the door.

I have to ask. "Are you going to tell Dad?" I blurt.

Lara looks at me, unblinking. The corners of her mouth do a smug little lift, but it would be lying to call it a smile. "I think not," she says, and I notice her free hand is stroking the mink pelts. But before I can thank her, she adds two more words that chill me to the bone. "Not yet."

As soon as the door shuts behind Lara, Cat mutters something in Spanish. Her mom is Guatemalan, and Cat speaks Spanish fluently. I don't understand the words — I take French in school — but there's no way to miss what she means. She's as freaked out as I am.

If Nelson, or even Chris the maintenance guy, who sometimes comes in here to make private phone calls to his girlfriend, had caught us in these costumes, they would have thought it was hilarious. The senior employees — Mr. and Mrs. Chen, or Loretta and Sadie, the elderly seamstresses who work with Nelson — might not have approved, but they would have turned a blind eye. Joyless never sets foot in the workroom. The only person in all of Cinderella Cleaners who would get us in trouble is Lara. So wouldn't you know she's the one who walked in on us.

"I can't afford to get fired," says Cat, her dark eyes worried.

"Neither can I."

"Are you kidding me? Your father owns the place. No way is he going to fire you." Cat pulls the granny dress over her head.

I wish that were true, but I've been on probation ever since the Halloween costume fiasco. How could I go and do something so stupid?

Well, no use beating myself up over something it's too late to change. I just have to be extra-good from now on . . . and hope Lara will keep our secret.

After work every day, I help out with the closing routine and then Dad and I go home together. It's so quiet when all the machines are shut down for the night, and the lights in the workroom snap off one by one. Usually I enjoy the supercharged silence — it reminds me of the hush that falls over an audience when the houselights go down, what my stagestruck mom used to call "magic time." But tonight the silence just makes me nervous.

As Dad locks the front door and walks me out to his car, with one arm draped proudly over my shoulder, all I can think of is how disappointed he'd be if he knew I was trying on customers' clothes. Again.

I really am going to stop doing this. Really, really, really.

Besides, I won't need to, I think as Dad drives the familiar route back to our house. I'll have a *real* costume soon, in *The Snow Queen*!

Well, I hope I will, anyway. Ms. Wyant didn't make any promises. And I didn't stay for the rest of the auditions, so someone might have been fifty times better than I was. I hope Jess and Riley get cast in the parts that they wanted. And am I a terrible person for hoping that Kayleigh gets cast as Third Villager? She doesn't have to get stiffed altogether. Just stuck in the chorus instead of the lead, so her swelled head can shrink down a few sizes.

Not that she won't still be cheerleading captain. How did I *know* Lara had been a cheerleader, too? It's the attitude. That "I'm on top, you're on the bottom" disdain. In my mind, I hear Lara's voice again, dropping the words like two stones down a well:

Not.

Yet.

If I'm ever cast in a play as a Russian spy, I will know just who to channel.

• • •

As Dad and I walk from the car to our house, I remind myself, *Think of good things. No Lara. No Kayleigh. No Fay.*

But my stepmother is hard to ignore. There she is, big as life and twice as blond, taking a rotisserie chicken out of the microwave where she's just warmed it. She's wearing the red pantsuit and patterned silk scarf she wore to her real estate office. Dad goes over to give her a kiss, and without even thinking, I lower my eyes.

They've been married three years now, and I still can't help feeling that Fay doesn't belong in our family. It may not be fair, but it's true. Especially since she always gives me the impression that I don't belong in hers. Ashley and Brynna are her daughters, and I'm just this extra encumbrance that came with my dad, like the not-your-style belt that comes free with a new pair of slacks.

"Hang up your coat," Fay tells Dad, as if he wouldn't think of that all by himself. "You, too," she says, turning toward me. "I need a hand with this salad."

And a nice warm hello to you, too, Fay. How was your day?

But I hang up my coat and join her in the kitchen. I washed my hands before I left the cleaners, but the dry-cleaning smells are hard to scrub off, so I do it again. Fay's left a bag of romaine, Parmesan cheese, and croutons on the counter, so she must have a Caesar salad in mind. Fine with me — it's one of my favorites, and easy to make.

I rinse and chop up the lettuce, putting it into the salad spinner. When I was little, I used to beg Mom to let me do this part. I loved the way the whole spinner would wobble around on the counter when I let go of the handle, and I'd pull off the top to watch while it was whirling so fast that the lettuce all stuck to the sides, like the Gravitron ride at Wildwood Amusement Park.

I empty the lettuce into a bowl, sprinkle on croutons and Parmesan, and take Caesar salad dressing out of the fridge. It's creamy and thick. As I'm thumping it out of the bottle, I hear Brynna's voice rise in a whine.

"Mo-om! She's wrecking the salad!" Brynna is standing right inside the doorway, pointing at me as if I just committed a crime. Even her blond pigtails, sticking out over her ears, look like they're accusing me.

Fay turns to look. "Oh, for the love of — Diana, you know the girls hate Caesar dressing. Why couldn't you just leave it plain so they can use Thousand Island?"

Because it's a *Caesar* salad, not a Thousand Island salad.

"I'm sorry," I say. "I forgot."

"She *always* forgets," Ashley says, fluffing her hair. "She's a dumb-butt."

I swing my head around. "Actually, I'm not a dumb-butt. I'm a pretty smart butt, and if you've got something to say to me, say it to *me*, not your mother."

"Diana!" Dad's voice is sharp. "That's enough of that." He moves right behind the twins, standing with one hand on each of their shoulders. Both girls have their arms folded over their chests, so the three of them look like a wall.

"I said I was sorry," I say, feeling hurt.

"You did. And then picked a fight over nothing," says Dad.

"You see?" Fay says to him. "That's just what I'm talking about."

Without a word, I take down another salad bowl and fill it with lettuce, croutons, and shredded Parmesan. I set it down right in front of the twins' dinner plates with a bottle of Thousand Island right next to it. No one says thank you.

I'm still thinking about the unfairness of this as I rinse off the plates after dinner and load them into the dishwasher. Four of them fit neatly into one row, and the fifth has to go on the other side by itself. That must be my plate.

Suddenly I feel like I don't get along with *anyone*. Okay, Jess and Will, but I'm having issues with Kayleigh, with Lara, and now with my whole family. It was bad enough when I just had problems with Fay and the twins, but I can't count on Dad to take my side anymore. It's a really bad feeling, like there's no one at all in my corner.

The phone rings. It's probably one of Fay's clients, but she's in the dining room, helping the girls with their spelling homework. Dad's watching the news.

I pick up the receiver and say, "Donato residence," as Fay's taught me to do in case it's a business call.

"Hello, Donato residence," answers a gravelly voice I'd know anywhere. It's my grandfather!

"Papa!" I cry in delight. Fay looks up from the table, and I hear Dad click off the TV in the living room, getting up from his chair.

"Would this be *Diana* Donato?" my grandpapa says. "'Cause I don't want to talk to the residence."

"How are you, Papa?" I say. I can feel a smile spreading across my face. "How is Nonni? How's Florida?"

"Fine, fine, and fine. Well, Florida's a little bit boring — all this crazy sunshine all day — so we thought we'd come up for Thanksgiving."

"Really?" I gasp.

"Didn't I say? I just said."

"*What* did you just say?" asks Dad, who's picked up on the other extension.

"They're going to come up for Thanksgiving," I bubble. I notice Fay fighting a frown, which makes this even sweeter.

"That's great, Pop," says Dad. "Did you find a flight?"

"Found it and booked it. I *wanted* to just show up on your welcome mat and ring the doorbell, but your mother insisted on giving some notice, the spoilsport. We fly into Newark at seven on Friday night."

Friday night? That's the day after tomorrow! Now I'm grinning ear to ear.

Finally, something to celebrate!

Chapter Four

I'm thrilled about seeing Papa and Nonni on Friday. But as soon as Dad hangs up, Fay starts in on how inconsiderate it is just to pop in on us like this.

"Did they ever consider that we might have Thanksgiving plans with *my* family?" she asks, joining Dad in the living room. Ashley and Brynna turn to watch.

"Well, we don't," says Dad. "It's just us chickens, and my parents haven't visited in a long time. I'm really looking forward to having them here."

Me, too, I think, closing the dishwasher, but I know better than to speak up when Fay and Dad are bickering.

"Are they planning to *stay* here?" asks Fay. "For how long? Thanksgiving's a whole week away, and it's a workweek. A busy one. I've got client appointments for days; I won't have time to play hostess."

While Dad explains patiently that Papa and Nonni have already taken a room at the Holiday Inn, though of course they'd be *welcome* to stay here, I head up the stairs. I can only deal with Fay's sniping for so long, and I need to get started on homework.

My social studies teacher, Ms. Pham, gave us the assignment of choosing a local place name and researching its roots. She explained that early settlers brought names from their home countries (New Jersey is named for a region in England, and so is New York), or named places for natural features (like Riverdell), or borrowed from Native American words like *Manhattan* (once called Mannahatta).

Ms. Pham also told us her last name is a Vietnamese version of a Chinese word that means "beekeeper." She told me that Donato means "gift" in Italian — from the same root as *donation*. Who knew?

I log on to my laptop, which has a new screen saver photo of all of my friends dressed up in their Vampire Prom Halloween costumes. Will looks extra handsome, but very self-conscious, like he can't believe that he's wearing this costume in public. I smile, and then log on to Google.

Here's a small sampling of place names you'll find in New Jersey: Tenafly, Netcong, Hopatcong, Ho-Ho-Kus, Hackensack, New Egypt, Plumbsock, East Orange, Nutley, Porchtown, Bivalve, Succasunna, Piscataway, Egg Harbor City, and Batsto. Not to mention my favorite, Buttzville.

It's easy to figure out how Ocean City or Beaver Lake were given those names, but what about Little Silver? Was somebody broke? What was so joyful on top of Mount Joy? And what on earth happened in Cheesequake?

I have to find out, so that's the name I decide to pick for my assignment. I Google the name and read about how it might have come either from a Lenni-Lenape word for "upland village" (*cheseh-oh-ke*) or because there's a geological fault line under the Cheesequake Marsh, and the earth "might have trembled like cheese" during an earthquake. I'm taking notes and grinning when my phone rings.

It's Jess, of course. She calls every night before bedtime. Before she can say anything, I ask her a question. "Since when does cheese tremble?"

"What are you talking about?" asks Jess.

I start telling her that I'm researching the deep roots of Cheesequake, New Jersey, for Ms. Pham, but she cuts me off. "Don't you want to hear about Kayleigh's audition?"

Oh, right. "I don't know. Do I?"

"She sang 'Memory' from *Cats*," says Jess.

"Really? I thought she'd sing something by Taylor Swift."

"Nope," says Jess, and she launches into a hilarious imitation of Kayleigh warbling *All alone in the mooooonlight . . ."*

When I'm done cracking up, I ask, "How did you do?"

"Okay. I went kind of off-key at the end. The Court Jester's not really a big singing role, but of course Ethan wants that part, too. And he read really well."

"I'm sure you were better," I tell her loyally.

"Well, yeah. But he's typecast. Hey! Jason just texted me about going to Homecoming with us!"

I sigh. Homecoming. In all the excitement of Papa and Nonni coming, I'd forgotten about the deal I made with Dad. I hate to break the bad news to Jess, but I have to. I take a deep breath and tell her that I won't be able to go if I'm cast in *The Snow Queen*.

"Are you kidding?" she gasps. "Why not?"

"Dad said I have to work Saturdays if I take off work during tech week. So it's either Homecoming or *Snow Queen*. Which would you want to do?"

"Both," says Jess. "Duh. I mean, that doesn't sound like your dad at all. That sounds like Fay."

"He's getting more like her," I tell her gloomily. "It must be rubbing off."

"Don't say that. Your dad is the best," says Jess. Her parents have been divorced for most of the time that I've known her, and her mom always seems to be mad at her dad about something or other.

We chat a bit longer, about family Thanksgiving plans — hers are still up in the air, but she's thrilled to hear Papa and Nonni are coming — and Jason. And getting together tomorrow night to work on our biology project, and Jason, and who's going to be at auditions tomorrow, and Jason. And did I mention Jason? Finally I hang up the phone and dive back into Cheesequake.

• • •

57

The next night at dinner, when I ask permission to go study at Jess's, Fay tells me I can't.

"We're low on groceries and I'm going to ShopRite. You need to stay here and watch the girls."

"What about me?" says Dad. "I can look after these characters." He reaches to ruffle Brynna's hair, and she ducks away from him.

"You're coming with me," says Fay. "My back's acting up and I can't carry heavy packages." Funny the way her back acts up whenever she wants someone else to do something for her.

"Take Diana," says Dad. "She can help you at the store, and then you can drop her at Jess's house on the way home. I'll help you unload. Problem solved."

Fay doesn't look pleased, but she has to admit it makes sense. So do I, though I don't really relish the one-on-one time in the front seat of Fay's SUV. Dad probably knows this, and thinks it's a bonding experience. He's clever that way.

The ShopRite is only a few blocks away, so we don't have to say very much on the drive. At least Fay has enough sense not to complain about Papa and Nonni's surprise visit; she knows I adore them. Instead, she asks me how my French class is going.

"Okay, I guess."

"Good." Conversational duty over, Fay flips on the radio. Fine with me, even though it's a really bad country station. But as soon as we park and get out of the car, I spot the last person I'd want to see when I'm out with my stepmother: Will!

He works at ShopRite part-time as a stock clerk, but I didn't know Thursday evenings were one of his shifts. But there he is, pulling on his jean jacket as he heads toward an idling Mustang.

Maybe he won't see me, I think hopefully, but of course he does. He lifts his hand in a wave and comes over to greet us.

Us. "Hi, Will," I say, trying hard not to squirm. "This is my stepmother, Fay. This is Will Carson. He goes to my school." I can feel myself starting to blush. There's no *way* I'd ever want to tell Fay about my complicated relationship with Will.

"Nice to meet you," says Will. He nods politely.

Fay looks from him to me. "Are you two friends?"

I squirm.

Then the Mustang turns off and Will's father gets out of the driver's seat. Now I'm completely flustered. Will's dad is such a cool guy — he's a sound engineer for big pop stars, like one of my favorites, Tasha Kane. And before that, he worked as a rock 'n' roll drummer. He's wearing a hip leather jacket with jeans and black cowboy boots. If it weren't for his beard scruff and designer glasses, he could probably pass as Will's much older brother.

"Hi, Diana," Mr. Carson says with a warm smile. "This must be your mom."

"Fay's my stepmother," I mutter as they shake hands. Will shoots me a look of sympathy, and I realize something that I've never noticed before: In the three months I've known him, he's never once mentioned his mother. Do he and his big brother, Steve, live alone with their dad? Are his parents divorced, and if so, is his mom still a part of the picture? Or might we have something really big in common?

I'll have to figure out some way to ask him that doesn't put Will on the spot. But not now. Fay is chatting away with his father in the artificially friendly manner she puts on with her real estate clients. I wish I was anywhere else on the planet.

"So what are you doing for your bio project?" Will asks me, and I'm grateful for the distraction.

"Jess and I are making a poster on plankton tonight," I say. "How about you?"

"I wrote a song. It's about photosynthesis."

"Really?" I grin. "That's so cool!"

"Mr. Stannus will probably flunk me," says Will, and his father turns to us.

"You better finish recording it, pal," Mr. Carson says. "You don't get A's for effort." He claps Will on the shoulder. "Good to see you, Diana. Nice meeting you, Kay."

"*Fay*. Like Tina Fey, with an *a*, not an *e*," Fay corrects him. She's trying to sound like she's kidding, but I know she's not. She can't stand it when people forget her name. But she doesn't stop smiling till Will and his father get into their car. I can tell what she's thinking: You never know when someone might need a real estate agent.

We go into the store and load up on staples, and Fay drops me off in front of Jess's house.

"Don't stay too late. It's a school night," she warns as I unbuckle my seat belt.

If it weren't, would I be about to go make a science poster? But I let it slide. I'm just glad to be at the Munsons', my second home.

Jess and her kid brother, Dash, are both in the kitchen, serving themselves ice cream.

"Pull up a bowl," says Jess. "There's Rocky Road, Caramel Swirl, and Chocolate Chip Mint."

"Yum!" I say, scooping a little of each flavor into my bowl. "Is your mom at work?" Mrs. Munson is a nurse at the local hospital.

Jess shakes her head. "Upstairs changing. She's on night shift tonight." Jess turns to Dash to see her brother licking Chocolate Chip Mint off the ice cream scoop. "Dash!" she shrieks. "Did I say I was done with that? Gross!"

"Not as gross as you," Dash says, dropping the scoop on the counter and sprinting from the kitchen with his loaded bowl.

"Pick that up!" Jess yells after him. "I'm not the maid!"

"Quiet down there!" Mrs. Munson calls down the stairs.

"Sorry!" Jess yells. Scowling, she takes a wet paper towel and soaks up the green ice cream drippings, then puts the scoop into the dishwasher while I cover the ice cream containers and put them back into the freezer. "Let's go work in my room, where we won't have to look at my brother," she says. I nod. Ashley and Brynna are pretty annoying, but Dash Munson is in a class by himself. We pick up our bowls and head upstairs.

I'm not allowed to bring food up to my room, but the rules at the Munsons' are looser. As long as you pick up after yourself, Mrs. Munson is pretty hands off. Maybe it's a single mom thing.

Which reminds me, I want to ask Jess what she knows about Will's mom. I wait till we're inside her room with the door shut for privacy. I love Jess's room. It's as cluttered as mine, but while my walls are covered with Broadway show *Playbills* and clothing accessories, hers are a shrine to everything Jonas. I notice that one of her JoBros posters has four heads instead of three: She's taped a photo of Jason between Joe and Nick. Our code name for him is 4-J, for Fourth Jonas, but I didn't know Jess was taking it quite so literally.

"Cute, huh?" says Jess, and I nod.

"Speaking of boys, do you know anything about Will Carson's mother?"

Jess smiles. "Speaking of cute boys? That one of us *likes*?"

I sigh. Do we have to go through this *again*? "Are his parents divorced?"

"I *think* so," Jess says. "But I'm not really sure."

"Did his mother stay in New Mexico when they moved here?"

"Ask Will. Once you start holding hands, you're allowed to converse." I'm about to protest — we held hands only *once* — but Jess changes the subject. "I wish *my* dad would move to New Mexico. He wants Dash and me to stay with him over Thanksgiving. My mom says no way."

It must really stink having parents who don't get along. Fay and Dad may bicker, but Jess's parents can't stand to be in the same *state*. (Her dad lives in Connecticut.) I'm trying to think of the right thing to say, but Jess changes the subject again. "So you like my 4-J poster? Isn't it awesome? Jason's mom took that photo of him in Barbados last winter. He said their hotel cost mad bank." She's off on a Jason monologue again. For the next twenty minutes I don't get a word in edgewise, except to say, "Shouldn't we at least *start* on our posters for bio?"

The next morning is Friday. Jess and I practically gallop up Underhill Avenue, with our science posters flapping like sails. This morning *The Snow Queen* cast list will be posted on Ms. Wyant's door, and we can't wait to see who got what role.

It's always smart not to get your hopes up too high, but I can't imagine why Ms. Wyant would have dangled the thought of a solo in front of me if she didn't want me to play the Enchantress. She wouldn't put me through the motions of asking my dad for permission, and then turn around and not cast me. Right?

Or would she? Anything's possible when you're doing a play.

As for Jess, she's convinced herself that Ethan's going to be cast as the Court Jester. She feels like she flubbed her singing audition. So she's really worried she won't get a part, or will be stuck in the chorus of townspeople with all the sixth graders. I tell her that's ridiculous, but like I said, anything's possible. So we're both pretty nervous.

When we get to the hall outside Ms. Wyant's classroom, there's already a cluster of people gathered. Everyone is jostling to see the piece of paper posted to the wall. I spot Riley Jackson, bending to look for his name. He raises a fist in the air and pumps it three times, saying, "Yes!" So at least *he* got cast.

Jess turns to me, still breathing hard from our sprint, and says, "Love you whatever."

"Me, too," I say, hugging her. "Break a liverwurst."

"Yuck!" she says, wrinkling her nose. "Break a Lifesaver. Lime." And we both rush to look at the cast list.

The first thing I spot is my name, halfway down:

THE ENCHANTRESS .... Diana Donato

66

Before I can even react, I hear Jess squeal, "I got it!" She points.

There it is, in Ms. Wyant's signature purple ink:

COURT JESTER ....Jessica Munson

We slap five and hug. Riley says, "Way to go, Jess!"

I look back at the top of the cast list. Riley is King. I turn to him, smiling, and say, "Riley, she got that one right. You rule!" Riley grins back at me.

Jess says, "Look at this, though," and points at Ethan's name. He's playing the part of Crown Prince. And then we both spot the deal breaker, in royal purple:

SNOW QUEEN .... Kayleigh Carell

So much for letting some air out of Kayleigh's swelled head. She's not only the lead; she's the *title*. She's going to be lording it over the rest of us worse than ever.

But even that can't burst the bubble of happiness I get just from knowing that I'll get to be in a play again, with Jess and Riley and Ethan and . . .

Just then, Ethan pushes his way through the crowd.

"Jessica *Munson*?" his voice booms. I turn and he's clutching his heart. "*Munson* is playing the Jester? What is this, typecasting?"

"You just didn't rate," Jess grins.

"Hey, I'm the Crown Prince. You work for *me*, Jess-ter," says Ethan.

"I work for King Riley. You're just his brat son," Jess retorts. "You know, the one who's *not funny*."

I grin. It feels great to be back in the Drama Club gang, and I realize how much I missed being part of the action this fall. Even shy Will is going to be part of the team, since he's signed up to run sound.

Of course, getting to play the Enchantress *does* mean I'll be working at Cinderella Cleaners every Saturday, starting tomorrow. So there goes attending the Homecoming game.

Jess thinks of it at the same moment as I do. She turns to me, frowning.

"Diana, I guess this means . . . you have to work at the cleaners tomorrow?"

"On Saturday?" Riley says, and Ethan says, "No way. On Homecoming?"

"Yes way," I tell them. "My dad told me I had to pick one or the other."

"Harsh," Riley says. "But I'm glad you chose the holiday show."

So am I! Even if Kayleigh the Snow Queen has a giant-size chip on her shoulder.

Snow *Queen* . . . Wait a second. I turn toward Ethan, grinning. "So Prince Ethan, does this mean that Kayleigh's your *mother*?"

"Hey," Ethan shrugs. "At least I don't have to kiss her. Speaking of which —" He turns, running his eyes down the cast list. "Who's Marisol Martinez?"

"I am," says a voice right behind us. "Could you guys move over so I can see?"

"Sorry," says Riley, stepping aside to make room for a petite, bright-eyed girl with shiny black hair.

I've seen her before; she's in seventh-grade chorus. But apparently neither Riley nor Ethan has noticed her, because they both react like cartoon characters. You can practically see their eyes go *BOING!*

Well, she *is* really pretty. And I know she can sing, because she had a solo in the spring concert last year.

"Oh, cool, I got in!" she exclaims, looking overjoyed.

"So did we," Ethan grins. "I'm your prince."

"Excuse me, I might lose my breakfast," says Jess.

"If you have to hurl, use your hat," Ethan says, and Jess sticks out her tongue. So does he. They look like a couple of six-year-olds.

"Hey, I'm Riley," says Riley, and Marisol blushes.

"I know," she says. "You were great in *Our Town*. And *My Fair Lady*." She dips her head, looking a little embarrassed at blurting so much, but Riley is eating it up with a spoon.

"Thanks, Marisol," he says with his million-watt smile. "See you at rehearsal."

"Yeah, I'll see you, too," Ethan adds, and Jess rolls her eyes.

Somehow I manage not to run into Kayleigh till lunchtime, when Jess and I sit at our favorite table with Sara and Amelia. Ethan's been eating lunch with us ever since he dumped Kayleigh, and Will sits here, too, when he's not doing extra band practice. Riley usually sits with a bunch of his friends from the track team, but today he joins our table. We're all gabbing excitedly about our roles in *The Snow Queen*.

"I can't wait for rehearsals to start," Riley says.

"Me, too," says Ethan, and Jess says, "Me three."

"I don't get it at *all*," says Amelia, who would play soccer 24/7 if she could. "My mother is making me be in *The Nutcracker*, and I've got to tell you, those rehearsals are like watching paint dry. For *hours*." She jabs her fork into a fish stick.

"*The Nutcracker*?" Riley asks, sounding impressed. "I didn't know you did ballet."

"I don't," says Amelia. "My sister does. My mother dragged me to ballet classes for years, but I hated it. I went to the tryouts just to make her happy, and now I'm stuck playing a windup toy."

"No kidding," says Riley.

Amelia nods sourly. "A harlequin doll."

"That sounds really fun," I say, trying to picture the way the windup doll moves in her harlequin costume.

"I wish I could study ballet," Sara says, unscrewing

71

the top from a thermos of mulligatawny soup from her family's restaurant, Masala. "My grandmother made me take classical Indian dance instead."

"And you're fabulous at it," I tell her, remembering our tryouts for the Tasha Kane video. "You should have tried out for *The Snow Queen*."

"Oh, please," Sara shudders. "I get stiff as a board whenever I have to say lines."

"So does Kayleigh, and she got the lead," Ethan says.

Jess cracks up and slaps him five. "Burn!"

"You see? I am *so* funny," Ethan says. "Speaking of Her Royal Kayleighness . . ." He lifts his chin toward the cafeteria entrance, where Kayleigh has just made an entrance that ought to win her a Tony award. Savannah walks two steps behind her. Even though she's clutching a pink-and-white lunch tote and Kayleigh is wearing jeans and a striped tee from Aeropostale, somehow Savannah gives the impression she's holding the train of Kayleigh's gown.

Of course they come right to our table.

"Look at this," Kayleigh simpers. "My whole royal family. And you, too, Diana."

Right. Me, too.

"It's going to be so fun," Kayleigh goes on. "See you all at Homecoming tomorrow, right? I can't wait to see the varsity cheerleaders. I heard their float is *fantastic* this year. Hey, don't forget to wear all blue and white!"

Does she think she's the only person who knows our school colors?

Jess is right on my wavelength, as usual. "Kayleigh, thank you *so much*," she says solemnly. "I was planning to dress in bright orange."

"Like your hair?" sniffs Savannah.

Kayleigh shoots her a look that says *I can handle the likes of Jess Munson without your help, thank you.* Savannah shrinks back.

"There's no need to be so *sarcastic*," sniffs Kayleigh. "I know you're just jealous. And that is so sad."

I would never admit it to Kayleigh, but I *am* a little bit jealous. I wish I could go to the Homecoming game and watch Will marching in the parade. And I wish I could have tried out for the part Kayleigh got, so I could rehearse every day with my friends, instead of just coming in during the very last week.

But I'm not complaining. Especially not today. Because right after work, Dad and I will be driving to the Newark airport to pick up Papa and Nonni!

I love driving out to the airport. It's only about twenty minutes away, but the route takes you up and over the Meadowlands salt marshes on a long, arching bridge. You can look down at the docks of Port Newark and see all the barges and shipping cranes lined up like huge metal dinosaurs. There are train yards and radio towers, and there's always a jumbo jet angling down over the highway just as you drive into the airport, so close that it looks like it's going to land right on the roof of your car.

Sure enough, there's a British Airways jet coming in now. I hold my breath as the engines scream over our heads. Did that just fly all the way over from *London*? How cool! I imagine all the sophisticated people on board, and wish I were among them, practicing my English accent.

We park in the short-term lot and walk into the terminal. As Dad looks at the overhead monitor, checking to see that the flight from Miami's on time, I swivel my head to check out all the different outfits. All around us, brightly dressed people zip past with wheeled suitcases, talking on cell phones. I see clusters of men wearing African robes and women in saris and head scarves. It makes me yearn to take off on a trip.

We go to wait at the arrivals gate. It's really fun to watch all the reunions. There are uniformed limousine drivers holding up hand-lettered signs with names like Rahel and Alia, family members, a few eager boyfriends and girl-friends. One guy's clutching a pink paper cone full of roses, and I wonder who he's going to give them to, and what she will say. After a few planeloads of passengers come through, we start to see people with Florida tans, and I stand up straighter, craning my neck.

A moment later, I spot an elegant silver-haired man in a white linen jacket and turquoise polo shirt. He is giving his arm to a much shorter, rounder woman with white-streaked hair twisted up on her head. The familiar sight fills me with joy.

"There they are!" I point. Dad grins and steps forward, waving.

Papa spots us and flashes a smile so warm that I feel like the sun just came out. His eyes are the same blue as

Dad's, with a mischievous sparkle, like light playing over seawater.

"There's my *bella ragazza*!" he calls out, beaming.

It's the nickname he's had for me since I was born. It means "beautiful girl" in Italian, though Papa's accent is more Newark than Rome — he grew up in New Jersey.

Nonni was born in Sorrento, Italy, near Mount Vesuvius, but her family came to America when she was four. Now she gives Dad a big hug, then turns to me, gasping and touching a hand to her chest.

"Diana!" she exclaims, her tinge of an Italian accent coming through. Her speaking voice is like somebody singing. "Look at you, oh! You're so *tall*!"

"Never mind tall; is she stunning or what?" Papa says. "You are *stunning*, Diana. You look like a top fashion model!"

That's nonsense, of course — I look like a regular brown-haired thirteen-year-old girl — but it makes me blush anyway.

Papa kisses the top of my head, wrapping his arms around me in a bear hug until Nonni tells him, "Don't hog her, Luigi!"

"Your turn," Papa says with a wink. Nonni pulls me into a hug and I drink in her familiar smell — equal parts perfume and pizza — before I realize that she barely comes up to my chin. Has she gotten smaller, or have I just grown? I look over her head to see Papa clap Dad on the back.

"Frank," he says. "Good to see you, son." They embrace on one side, then the other, clasping each other's arms. My heart lifts at the sight. There's nothing like being surrounded by people you love.

"So." Papa takes a deep breath. "Back in Jersey. There's no place like home, am I right or right?"

"There's no place like family," says Nonni. "I've missed you so much!"

"Me, too," I say, squeezing her hand.

"Fay and the girls?" Papa asks, looking around.

"They're home making dinner," says Dad. "Do you need to pick up any luggage?"

Papa lays a hand on his arm and says in a you-ought-to-know-better tone, "I'm not a carry-on type of a guy." This is true. As long as I've known him, Papa has been what he calls "a sharp dresser." Maybe that's why he opened a dry cleaner.

"Besides that, your mother is *cooking*," Papa continues. "She packed a whole test kitchen."

"Oh, I did not!" Nonni says.

"Everything but the sink," Papa teases, and she says, "Luigi!"

Dad throws up his hands, smiling at me. "Say no more."

We pick up their matching red suitcases from a carousel. When I was little, I always wanted to hitch a ride on the conveyer belt. I'd love to find out what's behind those big rubber flaps where the luggage comes in.

Dad drives Papa and Nonni to the Holiday Inn where they're going to stay. It's the same hotel where I tried out as an extra in Tasha Kane's video, with glitzy elevators that glide up and down inside clear plastic tubes, and an atrium with potted palms and an indoor pool. Papa claims they decided to stay there because of the heated pool — "It's good for your Nonni's legs" — but I suspect that it's also to keep a safe distance from Fay and the twins. I can't really blame them — in fact, I'm half tempted to check in myself. I'd love to lie down on one of those neatly made beds, close my eyes, and just sleep straight through till tomorrow.

Papa notices. "This one's a sleepyhead, Frank. She's going to conk out before dinner."

"I'm not sleepy at all!" I protest, but Papa just winks.

"Night-night and white light," he says, just like he used to when I was a toddler.

What else can I say but "White light to you, too?"

"You see that, Teresa?" Papa says, turning toward Nonni. "Diana might be big and gorgeous, but she still remembers her Papa."

"Of course she does," Nonni says, smiling at me. "Who could forget you?"

It feels just like old times.

Chapter Five

The next morning is gorgeous. Even at eight in the morning, the sun feels unusually warm for November. It's a perfect day for a parade.

As Dad drives me to work, we pass a road crew truck filled with the long wooden sawhorses that will serve as crowd barricades. Seeing this, I feel a fresh pang of loss about missing Homecoming.

Four hours from now, people will be lining up along Main Street to watch the parade. If I squint my eyes, I can picture little kids sitting up on their parents' shoulders, eager teens waving Weehawken Blue Jays pennants, and loud jocks wearing blue-and-white face paint. Jess, Amelia, Sara, and the others will be standing in front of the Jolly Cow, chowing down on their sprinkle-dip twist cones as Will marches past with the band.

And where will I be? In the back of the cleaners.

I sigh as the car comes to a stop behind Cinderella Cleaners. It's enough to make a girl feel sorry for herself. I try to remind myself there'll be other Homecoming parades, but only one chance to perform in *The Snow Queen*. I had to choose one or the other, and I made the right choice.

But that doesn't keep me from feeling bummed out.

Cat is in just the same mood. As we stand in the locker room, hanging up our coats and pulling on our light green smocks, she talks about her best friend, Marina.

"She came over last night after dinner, and she was so stoked," Cat says as she shuts her locker. "All she could talk about was the Homecoming court, and how she can't believe she got chosen to crown them, and it's such a big honor, and how cool their float's going to look, and she can't *wait* to ride on it."

I have to admit, this is one of my top secret fantasies. Whenever my family watches the Macy's Thanksgiving Day Parade on TV, I imagine myself on a float filled with

Broadway stars, dancing and singing and waving to crowds, with a giant Snoopy or SpongeBob balloon bobbing overhead. Once, when I was little, Mom and Dad drove me into the city the night before to watch the crews fill the balloons with helium. The balloons are really, really big, and they look very strange when they're halfway inflated. I loved it.

"Marina is going to ride on a float?" I ask Cat a little enviously as I snap my own locker shut.

"Uh-huh, with the rest of the cheerleaders."

The rest of . . .

Her words sink in and I feel a wave of shock.

"You mean your best friend is a *cheerleader*?" I blurt.

Cat is clearly surprised by my tone. "Yeah, so? I have friends who do all kinds of sports. Jared's a wrestler, Elise is on varsity basketball —"

"I know, but cheerleaders are snooty and mean," I interrupt, thinking of Kayleigh and her cronies.

"Evil cheerleaders? That is such a cliché," says Cat, rolling her eyes. "Next you'll be telling me all kids who go out for Chess Club are nerds."

"Well, aren't they?"

Cat shoots me a look of disdain. "Girlfriend, there's plenty of things you can call me, but I'm *not* a nerd."

I stare at her, jaw dropped. "You mean . . . ?"

"State Federation semifinalist." Cat elbows me in the ribs. "Checkmate. Hey, is it true that all Drama Club members are weirdos?"

I make my best weird face, and she laughs at me. Maybe it won't be so terrible working on Saturdays.

The morning routine is a little bit different from the routine after school. Cat and I have to collect all the orders that were tagged for a Saturday pickup, and make sure they're all finished and on the conveyer belt. There are also a lot of new drop-offs, and I make more trips to the customer counter than usual.

I've been at work for a couple of hours when I notice an elderly man waiting in line. He's wearing a battered 1940s-style hat and frayed trench coat. His head is slumped so far forward I can't see his face, and he's swaying a little and muttering.

Miss MacInerny glances at him, concerned. Lara looks disapproving.

"Next!" Lara says harshly. "Sir. Sir! Can I help you?"

The man stumbles forward. "I don't have my ticket," he rasps, still not looking up.

Lara's frown deepens. "Vat is your name? I'll check the computer."

"My name? I forget. Maybe somebody back there can —"

Suddenly the last thing I'd ever expect happens. Joyless breaks into an ear-to-ear grin.

"Luigi!" she shrieks. "Oh, you had me going!"

The man straightens up, whips off his hat, and it's Papa!

I don't know which shocks me more, that Joyless saw through his disguise, or that I didn't. But weirdest of all is the fact that Miss MacInerny is . . . *smiling*.

So is Papa. "Boy, stay away for a couple of years, and nobody knows you from Adam," he grins.

"You nearly gave me a heart attack!" Joyless gasps.

"Don't kid a kidder," says Papa. "And who is this gracious young lady?" He's looking at Lara, whose frown has turned into an expression of frozen fear. I know just what she's thinking: Has she been rude to someone important?

Indeed she has!

"This is Lara Nekrasova," Joyless says. "Lara, this is Luigi Donato, our founder. It's so good to see you, Lou."

Papa nods back at Joyless, as if he's happy to see *her*, too. I try to keep my jaw from dropping. Then Papa turns toward me, winking. "*This* one, I know."

"Hi, Papa," I say, going over to give him a quick hug. I can sense Lara bristling behind me.

"Let me go get Loretta and Sadie," Joyless says.

But she doesn't have to. The news must have traveled with her shriek, because both white-haired seamstresses barrel in, followed by Nelson. Loretta and Sadie sandwich Papa in group hug. Happy exclamations of "I can't *believe* this!" and "Such a surprise!" fill the air.

"All my girls," Papa beams. "Feels like old times." Then he grins at Nelson. "Hey, look, it's the new kid I hired. How's the tailoring biz?"

Nelson steps forward, shaking his hand. "That raincoat could do with a few alterations," he deadpans.

"Goodwill's finest," says Papa, petting the lapels. "Bought it this morning."

"Pop, you're impossible," says Dad, who's just come out of his office.

"Just checking the welcome mat," Papa says, clapping Dad on the shoulder. "You've got a wonderful staff here, but this one" — he nods in Lara's direction — "gave me the big chill when she thought I was down-and-out. Counter service is respectful and friendly, no matter what."

I have to admit, I'm enjoying this.

"I vill do better next time," Lara says, dipping her chin.

"Cheer up, honey," says Papa. "You're the first face the customer sees. A bright smile like Diana's, it goes a long way."

Ouch. Did he really just say that? Lara glares at me like I'm an ogre.

"Diana does not work the customer counter," says Joyless.

"Why not? She'd be perfect," says Papa. I try not to squirm, but I'm secretly pleased.

"She's too young to run the cash register." Joyless's frown is returning. She looks like herself again.

"Rules." Papa gives a dismissive shrug. "She isn't too young to greet customers and do clothing intake."

"Pop?" says Dad, laying a good-natured hand on his arm. "You're not the boss anymore."

Papa clutches his heart. "Too true," he says. "When you're right, you're right. Can I go to the workroom, at least? Visit my old pals?"

"Of course," Dad says, flipping up a hinged section of countertop so he can pass. "But the Chens aren't working on Saturdays anymore."

"Who does emergency stains?" Papa asks.

"We pitch in. Or it waits until Monday," Dad says.

Papa nods, pausing in front of my cart to drop in his shabby coat. "Give this a dry cleaning and mark it No Pickup, To Go," he says. "Someone could use it. Warm lining."

"Will do," I say, rolling the cart toward the double doors. Papa holds one side open for me like an old-fashioned doorman. He looks right at home, and I smile, remembering how I used to visit him here in his kingdom when I was a little girl.

Then Papa swivels his head — we all do — as a red car peels into the parking lot. I watch through the big plate-glass window as the car comes to a stop. All four doors open at once, and out jump . . .

Four cheerleaders! They're all wearing blue-and-white varsity cheerleading uniforms. Despite what Cat said before, I instantly flash on Kayleigh Carell times four. Is this my personal nightmare, or what?

"Somebody's sure in a hurry," says Papa as all four girls push through the front door.

And then we see why. The girl in front, slender and pretty with coffee-toned skin, has a bright red stain right down the front of her blue-and-white uniform.

"Hi," she gasps, panicked. "Is Catalina James working here?"

I turn around to call Cat, but she's already come through the open door. "Marina? What's wrong, girl?" She spots the red stain. *"Ay, Dios mio!* What *is* that?"

"A cherry slushie!" Marina says, almost in tears. "Roxie was driving. She stopped short, the lid slipped, and it went all over my lap."

"I'm so, so, so sorry," says a curly-haired girl with car keys in her hand.

"It's so not your fault," says Marina as one of the other girls, tall with her hair braided into tight cornrows, pats Roxie's arm and says, "Really." The fourth girl — a petite blonde who reminds me the most of Kayleigh — is silent. Must be that cheerleader attitude I know so well.

"I can't believe this," Marina wails. "The Homecoming parade starts at noon, and I absolutely *cannot* be late for it. I've got the Homecoming crowns!"

That's right — Marina's the friend of Cat's who got picked for the crown ceremony. She can't do that wearing a slushie.

I look at the wall clock. It's ten forty-five. Even with one-hour service, noon is going to be tight.

"Don't worry," Papa says, taking charge. "You've got the Cinderella Cleaners dream team on the case. Right, Diana?"

I nod. Marina may be a cheerleader, but she's Cat's best friend, and she needs help. "Right!" I say, and we spring into action.

• • •

The first thing Cat and I do is tell Marina we'll take her back to the employee locker room.

"No customers behind the counter!" Joyless protests.

"Except in the case of emergency," Papa says, lifting up a hinged section of countertop so Marina can cut through the workroom. Score! Another small victory over Joyless. "You can wait here," Papa says to the other three girls. "Just relax. She'll be back in a flash."

If we weren't so pressed for time, it would be fun to watch Marina react to the sounds and smells I've gotten so used to. But Cat and I hustle her back to the locker room as fast as we can.

"Here, put on my smock for now," Cat says, unsnapping it quickly. "The sooner we get that uniform into stain removal, the better."

Marina nods. "Thank you so much. Both of you." She plunks down her oversize white purse and peels off her stained blue-and-white minidress. Underneath it, she's wearing a racer-back sports tank and bicycle shorts. We're about the same height, but I can't help noticing how strong she looks. Cheerleading must be good exercise.

90

"Sink's right over there if you need it, Ree," Cat says to Marina. As Marina goes off to wash her slushie-sticky hands, Cat passes me Marina's wet uniform. "Diana, please bring this to — that guy Lou is your grandfather, right? He's so chill! Oh, and see if there's something on the No Pickup rack that Marina can wear while she waits."

"Um," I say, feeling embarrassed. Cat gets it right away.

"Right, you're not allowed. No worries, I'll take this out to your grandfather, and I'll check out the clothing options on the way back."

So I hand the uniform over and Cat's out the door.

Leaving me alone with a *cheerleader*. A high school varsity cheerleader, no less — Kayleigh's holy of holies. It doesn't help that Marina's beautiful. She looks like Beyoncé. What do I say to her?

"Cat is the best," says Marina, dabbing her face with a wet paper towel. "You must be Diana, right? Cat talks about you all the time."

She does? I feel a flush of happiness. "You, too," I stammer. "She says you're on student council together."

Now why would Marina need to hear *that*? Or care?

Sometimes the things that come out of my mouth are ridiculous. But Marina doesn't seem to mind.

"Cat is the heart and soul of student council," she tells me. "She should be the one who's crowning the Homecoming king and queen. Maybe next year, when she's a senior. I bet she'll be valedictorian, too."

"Really?" I feel like I'm seeing a new side of Cat. Chess team . . . and now this? You've got to admit, the girl's full of surprises.

"And she won't dump a slushie all over herself. I still can't believe I did something so *dumb*," says Marina, shaking her head. She sounds just like me, when Lara caught me in that elf suit. "I mean, who drinks a slushie for *breakfast*?"

Actually, that sounds delicious. I love cherry slushies. And lime ones. And grape.

"Don't worry," I tell her, glad I can offer some help. "We'll get that stain out in no time at all. We do one-hour service."

"That's great, but we're supposed to report to our floats by eleven fifteen," says Marina, frantically checking her watch. "I don't want to make my friends late."

"Could you meet them there?" I ask.

She shakes her head. "I already begged them to go and sign in, but they won't leave without me."

They sound like true friends. I'm surprised to find cheerleaders acting so unselfishly. Could the other three girls be as nice as Marina? Even the blond one? It doesn't seem likely, but maybe Cat was right. Maybe I've been jumping to conclusions too much.

Marina's still talking. "Becca says we're a team and we can't do the routines until I get there anyway, so what's the point? But, you know, what's the point of us *all* being late? Our coach will be going ballistic."

Cat comes back in. "Okay, Grandpa Lou's treating the stain, but there's *nothing* to wear in No Pickup. Ree, we've got to get you into some clothes in the meantime, because Roxie and Becca and Sandy will not budge without you. And I can't see you up on the float in that hideous smock."

"Wait up," I say, suddenly thinking of something. "I just remembered I've got my gym clothes in my backpack. And we're pretty much the same size," I add shyly, glancing at Marina.

"That's perfect!" says Cat. "You rock and roll."

"That is so sweet," says Marina.

Well, sort of. As I open my locker, I remember my sweat shorts and tank top are *dirty* — that's why I was bringing them home for the weekend. Marina can't wear my nasty old sweats on a Homecoming float!

"You know what?" I tell her. "You're going to freeze in these. Why don't I give you the sweater and jeans that *I'm* wearing, and I'll put these shorts on instead?"

"But —" starts Marina.

"Diana's right," says Cat. "It's always way hot at the cleaners. Trade clothes, you guys."

"This is so unbelievably nice," says Marina. "The shirt off your back! And it's blue and white, too!"

"I'm in eighth grade at Weehawken Middle School," I tell her as we swap clothes. "My friends are all going to Homecoming, and I'm meeting them at the game after I get off work. I'm just sorry that I'll have to miss the parade."

"But *you* won't," Cat says to Marina. "We'll have your uniform cleaned and delivered by noon. Go up there, sign in, do your warm-up stretches, and we'll have you back in your dress before the first float leaves the parking lot. Cross my heart."

"You guys are awesome," Marina says, zipping herself in my jeans. They fit her perfectly. So does my blue-and-white-striped boatneck sweater.

"You're like twins!" says Cat.

Hardly. Marina is gorgeous, and I look like refried gym leftovers. But I'll be okay with my smock on over my tank top and shorts, except for my blue-and-white knee socks and Converses.

"Come on, quick," says Cat, grabbing Marina's arm and tugging her out of the locker room. "We gotta get you back into Roxie's car."

"Thank you so much, Diana!" she calls out. "I owe you one, big-time!"

Did I just make friends with a *cheerleader*?

Chapter Six

Papa takes charge of the stain removal operation. He stands at Rose Chen's Special Care station, nodding approvingly as he studies her tidy worktable and neatly labeled jars full of potions and powders.

"Rose knows what she's doing," he tells me. "She keeps a nice table."

He unrolls a section of shelf paper, setting the stained uniform on the clean surface. It reminds me of a doctor's examining table, and I half expect him to take out a stethoscope.

"Artificial coloring, that's very bad," he says, pulling on latex gloves and running his fingertips over the slushie stain. "It looks worse on the white, but this blue fabric's much more absorbent. We might need a two-pronged approach."

He examines Rose's jars, then reaches out for a clear semi-liquid.

"Step one," he says, unscrewing the lid.

"What is it?" I ask him.

"Not health food," says Papa. "But it does the trick."

I watch Papa dab the gelatinous liquid over the stain like a seasoned old pro, working slowly and carefully. It smells like nail polish remover. "Diana?" he asks. "Can I ask you a personal question?"

"Sure," I say.

"Where are your pants?"

I look down at my kneesocked legs, realizing the smock is so long that my gym shorts are almost invisible.

"Oh," I say, turning pink. "I lent Marina my jeans."

Papa looks at me proudly. "Now *that* is what I would call personal service." He finishes dabbing the stain. "Ideally, I'd leave this an hour, two hours, to soak into the fibers. But we've got a parade to catch, so. Here comes Door Number Two." He reaches for another jar. "This ought to lift it right out."

Papa sprinkles a white powder over the gel and starts scrubbing it into the seams with what looks like a long-handled toothbrush. There's a faint smell of citrus, like the rind of a freshly cut grapefruit.

"Nothing like old-fashioned elbow grease," he says, leaning over his brush. "So how do you like working here at the cleaners? It's good?"

"I love it," I tell him, and that is the truth.

"I'm so glad," Papa says. "We might not win Nobel Prizes for doing this kind of work, but you know what, Diana? Looking good makes people *feel* good, and that is a great gift to give. Maybe *they* win the Nobel Prize. Or the Homecoming trophy."

He sets his brush into a cleaning solution and pulls off his gloves, discarding them into a trash bin. "Ten minutes we'll give this. Get busy with something you've been putting off, so the time won't drag by."

I rack my brain. Is there any task I've been putting off?

Yes, in fact. I need to assemble that order of Santa and elf suits and get them all tagged and bagged for pickup. I don't want to jog Lara's memory more than I have to, so I've been waiting until she was away. No such luck, but I can't avoid it forever.

Just as Papa suggested, the job fills the time while we wait for the cheerleader uniform outcome. The Santa order has dozens of garments, and they've all been cleaned, except for a few that are still in the Tailoring section awaiting repairs — Nelson's been busy all week. The ten minutes go by in a flash, and so does the special care cycle inside the big metal cleaning machine. In no time at all, Cat and I are standing with bated breath, waiting for Papa to open its door.

"You girls ready?" he asks, and we nod.

Dad comes back to join us, jangling the keys for the Cinderella Cleaners delivery van. "Is it done yet?"

Papa unlatches the heavy door, releasing a twin scent of dry-cleaning fluid and grapefruit. He reaches into the barrel to take out the blue-and-white dress. His back blocks our view for a moment as he looks the uniform over.

"Did the stain come out?" Cat asks breathlessly.

Papa turns, holding the garment in front of his white shirt. "Spotless," he says with a satisfied smile. "I've still got the touch."

"Go, Papa!" I cheer, and he beams.

"You can take the old man out of the cleaners, but you can't take the cleaners out of the old man," Papa adds, beaming.

"Good for you, Pop," Dad says, patting his back. "One of the girls paid the bill in advance, so we're good to go. Their float's in the parking lot of Holy Cross Church, right off Main Street. Cat? Can you make the delivery?"

"You bet," Cat grins, taking the keys. "Let me just grab my coat."

"Can I go with her?" I blurt.

Dad frowns. "I don't see why a delivery job takes two people."

It doesn't, of course. But as soon as Dad said the word "float," just a second ago, I could picture the scene — all the trucks and floats lining up for the parade, the bagpipers and marching bands warming up.

I know there's no way I can watch the parade with my friends, but this would be *something*, at least. Maybe I'll even get to see Will in his band uniform!

"Why not?" Papa smiles. "I can stand in for both of these girls. I'm a working professional."

"That you are, Pop," says Dad. "And a pain in the neck."

"Oh, come on," Papa says. "It's how far away — fifteen minutes? They'll be back here before you can blink."

I'm starting to feel a little guilty. I know Papa likes to dote on me, but I wonder if I might be pushing my luck. "Dad's right," I say quickly, thinking about the Santa and elf suits that I just hung up. "I don't have to go. I promised I'd work every Saturday, and that's what I'll do."

Dad looks at me, his eyes twinkling like Papa's. "That's true, Diana," he says. "But I guess a delivery run *could* count as work."

What just happened? Did Dad change his mind?

"That's my boy," Papa says, clapping him on the back.

"Be sure you come right back," Dad says to Cat. "Don't you stay up there to watch the parade."

"I promise," Cat says. "We'll come right back."

"Dad, you're the best!" I exclaim, giving him a quick hug.

"Here," Papa says, folding the cheerleading uniform neatly and handing it over. "No bag; it should air. And drive carefully!"

"Always," says Cat. "But we've got to get going."

We hurry back into the locker room to grab our coats. I'm glad mine is long; it'll cover my bare legs better.

Cat looks at the clock as she zips on her leather jacket. "Twenty minutes," she says. "We'll just barely make it."

I'm closing my locker when I spot a big white slouch purse on the floor. "Hey, isn't that Marina's?"

"It sure is," says Cat. "Good eye. She must be freaking out that she left it here."

As I bend down to pick up the overstuffed purse, a wallet slides out on the floor.

"Oops," I say, picking it up. "She won't want to lose *that*."

"Here, toss it in," says Cat, holding the top of the purse open for me.

Something large and metallic catches our eyes. As we look into the open purse, both of us gasp at once.

Right on top are the Homecoming crowns!

Cat and I are on a mission. Those crowns *have* to get there before the Homecoming parade starts at noon, and so does Marina's cheerleading outfit! We strap on our seat belts — Cat's right, she's a really safe driver — and pull out into traffic.

"Got your cell phone?" asks Cat.

I nod and she gives me Marina's number. As soon as I dial it, I hear a Black-Eyed Peas ringtone go off in Marina's purse.

"Duh. Of *course* her phone is in her purse," says Cat, shaking her head. "Wait. Who came in with her? Try Roxie."

She gives me that number, and Roxie picks up on the very first ring with a breathless, "Hello?"

"Is Marina there?" I ask.

"*Yes!*" says Roxie, and I hear her call, "Ree! It's for you!"

Marina gets right on the phone. "Cat?"

"It's Diana. I'm with Cat. We've got your uniform *and* your bag," I say. "With the Homecoming crowns."

"Thank goodness!" Marina breathes. "I would be in so much trouble if those didn't get on the float. Where *are* you guys?"

"We're on our way in the dry-cleaning van," I tell her, and Cat calls out, "Underhill Avenue!"

"Underhill Avenue," I relay back. "And your uniform looks great. The stain is totally gone."

"You guys saved my life!" Marina cries. In the background I hear someone call, "Come on, Marina, *now*!"

"Are you close?" asks Marina, her voice sounding panicked. "We're supposed to be on the float getting ready."

"Less than five minutes," says Cat. "If we catch all the stoplights."

I look at the clock on the dashboard. Nine minutes till noon. This is going to be hair-trigger timing. Trying to stay calm for Marina's sake, I repeat Cat's words.

"Great," says Marina. "Can I just ask one more favor? Please leave the crowns inside my purse, okay? Don't let anyone see them. If our advisor finds out that I almost lost them, she'll —"

I hear her cover the phone with her hand, yelling, "Right there!" Then she gets back on. "I'm not kidding, Miss Doyne would go out of her mind. And the whole ceremony is sunk if I don't have those crowns."

"Got it. We'll be there super soon," I say.

"Thank you so much," she says gratefully. But just as Marina hangs up, the stoplight ahead turns to yellow.

"Ouch," says Cat, braking. "Come on, come on. Quick light. *Fast* light. Get it over with, light. Come on, we need some green here."

I start chanting with her, "Go, green! Go, green!" We sound like a couple of cheerleaders.

The light finally turns. "Will we make it?" I ask her.

"I *think* so," Cat says as we drive up the hill past Dogwood Avenue. The church parking lot where the parade is assembling is only two blocks to our left, but as we reach the crest of the steep hill, we both groan at once.

Of course there's a barricade. The main street is stopped for parade traffic, and there's a crowd spilling out along both sides.

"We better back up and cross over on Dogwood," says Cat. She looks in the rearview mirror, but it's too late: A pickup truck's pulled up behind us.

We're stuck.

"I don't believe this!" Cat moans. "We're so *close*!"

I look over my shoulder. "Can you back up, or —"

"I can't do anything," Cat says. And then she looks at me. "But *you* can."

"What do you mean? I can't drive!"

"You could bring it on foot," says Cat. "We're only two blocks away. You'd be there in three minutes."

I *could*, but I don't want to think about what Dad would say if I got out and went to the parade route — though of course that's exactly what I want to do! "I promised Dad I wouldn't get into any more trouble."

"I know, but we promised Marina, too. You heard what she said about needing those crowns. And besides, she's a *customer*," Cat says.

That's true. I can feel my heart starting to race. I can just hear what Papa would tell me to do: Put the customer first.

"I'd do it myself, but I can't leave the van," Cat says. "Please? She's my best friend."

And that seals the deal. If Jess needed me to stick my neck out for her, I wouldn't hesitate. I've already done it — I posed as a Foreman Academy student to get her cell phone back. I even took a Latin test for her!

"Okay, I'll do it," I tell Cat, unbuckling my seat belt. "I just hope they'll let me get through."

"They have to," she says. "I just hope you're on time. It's eleven fifty-five."

"I'm wearing my track shorts. I'll run like the wind." I peel off my coat, grabbing Marina's white purse and the cheerleading uniform. "I'll be right back. Don't go anywhere."

Cat snorts. "Like I've got a choice."

I jump out of the van. "Wish me luck."

"You're the best!" says Cat. "Do whatever it takes!"

I nod and start running. The strap of the heavy purse slides down my arm, and I cross it over my shoulder, messenger-style. With the cheerleader uniform tucked under my opposite arm, I feel like a quarterback making a break for the goalpost.

There's only one problem: The other team is a crowd of a few hundred people.

The whole parade route is crammed with Weehawken Blue Jays fans, with coolers and lawn chairs, and little kids and big dogs. An arch made of blue and white helium balloons stretches over Main Street, and people on both sides

107

hold up pennants and sheets lettered in spray paint: *GO TEAM!*

I haven't gone more than a few hundred feet when I realize I'll never be able to cover two blocks if I have to dodge through this crowd. I double back toward the parallel street we just passed, Dogwood Avenue. As I sprint past the Cinderella Cleaners van with its gold crown on the roof, Cat rolls down the window and asks, "Are you out of your mind? It's *that* way!"

"Too crowded," I pant, streaking past. I turn onto Dogwood, which is, thankfully, empty, and run pell-mell toward the steeple I see through the trees. *I can make it*, I think. *Almost there!*

Two blocks later, I turn to the right and charge into the church parking lot where the parade's lining up.

Not a moment too soon. As I skid into the lot, I hear the firehouse's noon whistle blow. It's answered by dozens of car horns.

The parade is beginning!

I'm in a panic. I know that the fire trucks always go first, then the bagpipe brigade, and next comes the . . . What? I swivel my head and see half a dozen floats lined

108

up in formation. They're all blue and white. Which one belongs to the cheerleaders?

Luckily, there's only one marching band, and I've arrived just as they're squaring up rank-and-file lines behind a big flatbed truck float that says CLASS OF 2011. I look down the rows of drums, clarinets, saxophones, trumpets, trombones — and there's Will with his silver euphonium!

I run toward him, gasping, "Which way are the cheerleaders?"

Will almost drops his horn as he gawks. It's hard to say which is more of a shock to his system — hearing me ask that question, or seeing me there in my gym shorts. But then he blinks and points up ahead. "Their float's in the front."

"Thanks!" I yell, galloping off toward the front of the line, which is already starting to move. But wouldn't you know it, a man in a coach's windbreaker and mirrored sunglasses blows his whistle at me, holding up his hand like a traffic cop.

"Parade personnel only!" he shouts, standing next to a row of sawhorses. "No guests past this point."

"I'm not a guest!" I tell him. "I've got to —"

But I don't get to tell him what I've got to do, because just at that moment, the drum major lifts his baton and the band starts to play. The combined sound of snare and bass drums, brass instruments, two hundred marching feet, and one eighth-grade euphonium totally drowns out my words.

I don't know what to do. The cheerleaders' float can't be more than a hundred yards from the spot where I'm standing. I can't give up now!

I stand breathing hard, with the coach's words echoing inside my head. *Parade personnel only.*

I'm holding a blue-and-white cheerleading uniform. What if I . . .

I don't even let myself finish that thought. *You can't,* says a stern voice inside my head. *You promised Dad you'd stop putting on customers' clothes! What would happen if you got caught?*

But another voice answers immediately. It's Papa's, and he's saying proudly, *That's what I'd call personal service.* And then I hear Cat's voice calling after my back as I run, *Do whatever it takes!*

To help her best friend. The way I would help Jess.

I don't have a moment to spare. The parade's already starting to move. Before I even know that I've made a decision, I'm stepping behind a parked school bus and pulling Marina's cheerleading uniform over my head.

Do whatever it takes!

Chapter Seven

The uniform's miniskirt just barely covers my shorts. I yank my wavy hair out of the ponytail I always wear at the cleaners and shake it loose. I hope I'll look different enough from the girl in gym shorts that the coach won't recognize me. I wish I had sunglasses I could put on, or *something*.

Maybe it will help if I come from a different direction. I run down the far side of the bus, then the next bus, and duck under the last of the sawhorses.

"Hey!" the coach calls out, and I hear his whistle blast over the thundering drumbeats. But I don't turn back. I just yell, "Missed my float!" and keep running as fast as I can.

As I speed past the Class of 2011 float, I hear a chorus of voices cheering. A boy yells out, "Looking good!"

Is he talking to *me*?

Then I realize: I'm *not* me. I'm dressed as a cheer-leader.

Wow! Does the uniform really make that much differ-ence in how people see you?

The next float ahead is low and wide, and it's being pulled by a pickup truck. It's covered with blue and white crepe paper flowers. There's a tall papier-mâché birch tree in the center, holding a nest full of soft-sculpture blue jays. Seated around the tree, on fabric-draped steps, are the var-sity cheerleaders. They're all wearing the same uniform I have on, and holding shiny gold pom-poms. As I sprint for the tailgate, the float lurches forward.

A redheaded cheerleader points, and the rest turn to stare at me. Most of them look completely confused — *Who is that, and why is she dressed like US?* But then I hold up the white purse.

"It's Marina's!" I shout.

Becca, the tall girl with cornrows who came into the cleaners with Marina, is the first one to recognize me. "It's Cat's friend!" she exclaims. "From the cleaners!"

"Diana, right?" cries Roxie, the girl with the curly hair who'd been driving the car. "Thank God you're here!"

I'm jogging alongside the float as it rolls slowly forward, trying to untwist the purse over my shoulder and toss it up to one of the girls.

But Roxie holds out her hand. "Jump on," she says.

I shake my head. "I can't do that," I pant.

She turns to her friends, saying, "Come on, you guys. Help her up!"

A cluster of arms reaches down, and somehow I manage to belly flop onto the back of the float. The cheerleaders help me up over the tailgate.

The boys on the float right behind us must think we're the best entertainment in town. They cheer, clap, and whistle as two of the cheerleaders bend down to straighten the flowers I squashed.

I get onto my knees, then up to my feet, with some help from Becca and Roxie.

"I'm so sorry we didn't get here a few minutes sooner," I gasp as Roxie helps me untwist the strap of the white purse.

"Are you kidding me? You're our hero!" says Roxie. "But we've got to sit down while the float is in motion. Strict rule."

"I can't stay on this float!" I say in a panic. "I have to get back to the van! Cat's waiting, and my dad —"

But before I can continue, an angry woman's face twists back through the passenger window of the pickup truck pulling the float.

"Sit DOWN, girls!" she shouts. "Safety first!"

"That's our coach," Becca hisses.

"Quick," Roxie says, pulling me onto the step right behind the fake tree and stashing the purse underneath it. "Keep your back to Miss Doyne!"

I sit down fast, in between Roxie and the blond girl who also came into the cleaners, the one I thought must be a snob.

"I'm Sandy," she tells me with a wide, friendly smile. She hands me two shimmery pom-poms.

"Thanks," I say uncertainly. I've never held pom-poms before, and they feel strange in my hands.

"Just in case," Sandy says as the float lurches forward again, rolling down the church driveway and out onto Main Street. The band music swells as the crowd cheers and claps on both sides of the street.

That's when it hits me.

I'm in the Homecoming parade!

On the cheerleading float!

I don't know whether to burst out laughing or burst into tears. Cat's stuck in traffic two blocks away, and three blocks beyond that is the Jolly Cow, where my friends have gathered to watch the parade go by.

What will they do when they see me up here?

What will *Dad* do when we're late getting back to the cleaners?

And where in the world is Marina? I practically killed myself getting her purse with the Homecoming crowns onto this float like she said, and she's nowhere in sight.

Then I get the surprise of my life. I hear Marina's voice, clear as day, saying, "Thank you, Diana."

Am I going crazy? Maybe the marching band music and crowd noise are giving me hallucinations.

I whip my head around, wondering if anybody but me heard her speak. Then I hear her again. "I'm inside the trunk," she says.

"What?" I must really be losing my mind.

"Of the tree," says Marina. "It's hollow."

"You're kidding!" I start to turn, but Roxie grabs hold of my shoulder.

"Be cool," she says. "That's where we hid her. Don't worry, we've got a plan. Wave to the crowd!"

Sandy passes a basket of blue and white wrapped taffy candies.

"No, thank you," I say, but she says, "For the kids." Oh.

So I sit there surrounded by varsity cheerleaders, waving and smiling and tossing out handfuls of blue and white wrapped taffy candies to scampering kids. If I wasn't stressing about how to swap clothes with Marina and get back to the delivery van before Cat freaks out completely, this would be actually . . . fun.

We pass under the high balloon arch, and the marching band's heart-pounding drums and jazzy brass make me wish I could get up and dance. It's my Macy's Thanksgiving Day Parade fantasy come to life!

Everyone's eyes are on us. Little girls flash starry-eyed smiles, calling, "Look, Mommy, *cheerleaders*!" and their older sisters shoot us looks of sheer envy. The boys in the crowd grin at us as if we're the cutest girls they've ever seen.

I'm not used to receiving this kind of attention, except maybe during a two-minute curtain call after a play — but that's different. Do cheerleaders really have this sway over people? No wonder some of them wind up getting swelled heads, like Kayleigh Carell.

Speaking of which . . .

Could those two blondes in identical pink and white parkas standing in front of the hardware store be anyone else but Kayleigh and Savannah? Their eyes are glued to the cheerleader float, but they haven't recognized me yet.

Well, why would they? Varsity cheerleaders are their superheroes, and I'm anything but.

Oh, this is too good. I reach into the basket and pelt them with blue and white candies, then wave my gold pom-poms and grin.

I don't think I've ever seen anyone's jaw drop so far, so fast.

"*Diana?*" gasps Kayleigh. Savannah just gapes. They swivel and stare as our float passes by. I keep waving my pom-poms, unable to stop smiling. Whatever else happens today, even if I get in trouble, it was totally worth it for this moment!

The parade's almost up to the Jolly Cow, where Jess's jaw is bound to drop, too, maybe even farther than Kayleigh's. She's been listening to me complain about cheerleaders for ages, and here I am dressed as one, having the time of my life.

There's only one problem. A few blocks past the Jolly Cow is the high school football field, where the Homecoming court ceremony will take place right before the first kickoff. I've got to get out of this cheerleading outfit before we get there, and get it back onto Marina. But how? We're on a parade float, surrounded by cheering crowds on both sides. Talk about no place to hide!

"Marina?" I say out of one side of my mouth while I smile and wave. "Can you hear me in there?"

"Loud and clear," says the birch tree.

"How are we going to trade clothes?"

"Don't worry, we worked it all out," says Marina. "At quarter past twelve the parade's going to stop to let traffic go through. After we do our routine —"

Wait up, did I hear that right?

119

"Our routine?" I repeat frantically. "What do you mean, 'our routine'?"

"Oh, you just have to do a quick cheer," Roxie says, waving to the crowd.

"Just follow what we do," says Becca. She's waving, too.

"It's simple," says Sandy, flipping her blond hair over one shoulder. "High V, broken T, candlesticks, split. Piece of cake."

High V, broken T, candlesticks, split?

These are words to strike fear through my heart. Half of them don't make sense. I can't *do* a split, not even close. And what in the world is a candlestick?

I've had to learn plenty of dance steps for musicals, and I even started ballet classes back in first grade, though I switched to tap after a year and never looked back. It's not like I have no extension at all. But there are people whose legs can go into a split, and I am not one of them.

Okay. So I'll be the "varsity cheerleader" with the stiff legs. But will I be the one who can't get a single thing right?

As our float glides past Neuhauser's Hobby Shop, Roxie explains that the first three are arm moves — arms up in a V (well, I can do *that*!), arms up to the sides with bent elbows (check), arms out in front like you're holding two candles (I think I can handle it).

"No jumps, because we're up here on this flatbed. Just keep smiling," she says as the truck rumbles over a bump. "Pom-poms high."

Becca teaches me the chant, which is simple. I've always prided myself on being a quick study at learning lines, and it's really short:

> *Hey, hey, Blue Jay fans,*
> *Yell it out and rock the stands!*
> *Let's go, let's go,*
> *Go, team, GOOOOO!!!*

Cool, fine, I've got it down. So I'll wave my pom-poms a few times, humiliate myself with a not-so-split, and we're done. "So that's all?"

"Uh-huh, and then we do a pyramid," Sandy says.

Um, just shoot me. "And where is Marina supposed to be?"

"Right in the center," she says. "On the top. But you won't have to do any flying dismounts. It's a modified."

Glad we got *that* straight.

I look up at the clock on the church steeple to see how much longer I have to live. It's fourteen past noon, and the minute hand moves. Our float slows and comes to a stop — right in front of the Jolly Cow!

Chapter Eight

Kayleigh and Savannah might not have spotted me right away, but it takes Jess about two and a half seconds. Her mouth forms a perfect O. I've rarely seen Jess Munson speechless, but this time she is.

"What the . . . ?" blurts Amelia, and Sara is so shocked she drops her ice cream cone. Ethan just hoots with loud laughter and points, jogging Riley's arm. Riley takes one look at me in my cheerleader dress and starts cracking up, too.

If they think I'm funny *now*, wait till they see me trying to cheer.

I can feel my face turning the color of a cherry slushie. The one consolation is that Will is safely behind the Class of 2011 float, wearing a euphonium harness and a foot-tall blue hat with an ostrich plume. He's in no position to laugh at me.

But I can't help wondering: *Would he?* Would he join Riley and Ethan in the making-fun squad, or would Will realize I was completely freaked out and embarrassed and give me a sweet smile that made me feel better about all this?

Somehow I think it's the second option. But I don't have time to think about that now. Our float has stopped moving, and my new cheerleader buddies are standing up tall with their pom-poms held under their chins.

I take a deep breath. I'm the star's understudy. I have to go on.

"You can do it, Diana!" I hear from the birch tree. And off we go.

Hey, hey, Blue Jay fans . . .

We hold our arms high in a V. The space on the flatbed is cramped, and we're practically shoulder to shoulder. Somehow I manage to avoid hitting Roxie and Becca in the face as I raise my arms, but my pom-poms are covering both of their faces.

Oops.

Yell it out and rock the stands . . .

Which move was next, broken T? Arms out and bent at the elbows. Oh. Not at the waist, at the *shoulders*. Well, too late now.

Let's go, let's go . . .

And here come the candlesticks. Arms out in front, shake your pom-poms. Woo-hoo! I got something *right*!

Go, team, GOOOOO!!!

Okay, folks, here goes nothing. Squeezing my eyes to a squint and doing my best not to wince, I slide down as far as I can toward the floor, one leg forward and one leg back. Only then do I realize the girls on both sides of me are doing *standing* splits, holding one ankle above their heads like gymnasts.

Oh.

As I stagger back up to a standing position, I see Riley and Ethan falling against each other with laughter. I'm blushing so hard I'm afraid I might faint.

And here comes my nightmare: the pyramid.

I was picturing the hands and knees 3-2-1 style of pyramid we do in gym class. But once again, cheerleading terms turn out to be different: This move is a *standing* pyramid. Three girls on each side form the bases, clasping their hands fireman-style in the center to make platforms, and two of the smaller girls climb up to stand on them, raising their arms as the watching crowd claps. My job, it seems, is to climb up between these two human towers and straddle them.

Right in the center.

With everyone watching.

I notice a man with a professional-looking camera on a tripod. He steps out in the street for a clearer shot. Perfect. Couldn't be better.

"Left foot on my leg," hisses Roxie.

"And right foot on mine," Becca says as I clamber up onto their bended knees, hoping I won't fall down on my face and pull everyone with me.

The crowd has begun to clap rhythmically. "Go-go-go-go!" they chant.

Was it Ethan who started this? I'm going to murder him.

If I survive, that is.

"Okay, now up to my shoulder," says Roxie. Her shoulder? I really don't see how that's possible. But I wedge my foot upward, grab hold of a hand on the opposite side, and swing my weight up. Somehow I land my other foot near enough to Becca's shoulder that she can duck down and get underneath it, helping me up.

The two girls in the second tier — Sandy and a dark-haired girl who looks a little like Sara — grab hold of my hands.

"You're doing great," Sandy says. "Now carefully pull yourself up to a standing position."

Is that all?

I take a deep breath, clutching their hands as I straighten up. It takes me a very long time, and I feel like I'm wobbling first to one side, then the other. I look down, dizzy. How did the floor of this float get so far away?

"You're there," Sandy says. "Now we're going to let go of your hands."

"You're *what*?" I gasp.

"So you can do a high V. We'll support you at the waist. Are you ready?"

No!

Gulp. "I guess."

They let go of my hands, moving their hands to both sides of my waist. From below I hear "Go-go-go-go!" I swallow hard and raise both arms high above my head in what I hope is a triumphant high V.

The crowd cheers and claps. And . . . it feels great. I'm beaming from ear to ear. I did it! I don't even mind when the man with the tripod tilts his camera upward to frame the whole pyramid, standing against the blue sky.

Now all I have to do is get down.

That doesn't go quite as smoothly, but somehow I manage to clamber and lurch my way back to the floor of the flatbed. Then all of us pick up our pom-poms and stand in a row for . . . Is it called a curtain call?

I hear people gasping and pointing at something behind us. Without breaking ranks, I manage to turn my head just enough to see that the blue jay nest in the tree is rising up and tipping forward, pushed up by hands hidden inside the tree trunk. *It's Marina!* I realize. The nest rains down blue and white glitter confetti. The crowd goes wild.

That's got to be the grand finale, right? But as we stand in a row with our pom-poms held up in the candlestick pose (thank you, Roxie!), two big "Blue Jays RULE!" banners unfurl from the guylines connecting the top of the tree to the cab of the pickup truck pulling our float. Everyone cheers their heads off.

Especially me, because all of a sudden, I get it. That enclosed triangle behind the two banners, with the birch tree at its point, makes a perfect dressing room!

"Quick!" Sandy tells me. "Duck under the banner!"

I do, just as Marina swings open a section of chicken-wire tree trunk and squeezes out. She looks a little rumpled, but otherwise fine.

"Good thing we built it hollow to rig that confetti trick," she whispers, shimmying out of my sweater. "But the girl who was supposed to be in there is half my size," she adds, stretching her long legs. "It was *tight*."

So is the triangle between the two banners. But some-how I manage to take off the cheerleading dress without bumping into either the tree or the banner. Marina pulls the uniform on over her head, and I put my sweater on over my tank top. The jeans are the hard part. There's barely time for Marina to wriggle them over her sneakers before we hear Roxie's hissed whisper, "Get *out*! The parade is about to roll!"

Marina looks at me, distraught, but I tell her, "It's fine. I've got my shorts on."

She nods, giving me a quick hug as she hands me my jeans. "You totally saved my life, Diana. Thanks a billion!"

Then she ducks under the banner on one side, rejoining the cheerleading squad, and I duck out under the other, jumping down off the float right in front of my friends. They cluster around me, exclaiming.

"Did I just hallucinate?" Jess demands. "What *was* that?"

"I just totally saved someone's life," I tell her, beaming from ear to ear.

"I dropped my ice cream cone when I saw you up there," says Sara.

"I saw that," I grin. "Sorry."

"Here, have a bite," says Amelia, holding out hers. "I think you earned it."

I take a big bite of Amelia's half-finished twist cone, turning to wave at the cheerleaders' float as the parade starts moving again. All my new friends wave back: Roxie, Becca, Sandy, and Marina, who, of course, looks right at home holding pom-poms. The switch has gone off smoothly, and unless you were really paying attention, you wouldn't know that Marina hadn't been there all along.

"Dude, you're the worst cheerleader *ever*," Ethan grins.

"Hey, let's see *you* do a standing split!" Jess says, swatting his arm. "Not to mention that pyramid thing. That was awesome!"

"How'd you wind up in that uniform?" Riley asks.

"I'll tell you guys later. I've got to get back to the Cinderella Cleaners van, quick." But just as I turn to start back along the parade route, the Class of 2011 float rolls past. Right behind that is the marching band!

"Sergeant Pepper alert!" Ethan yells.

The drum major's strutting and prancing with his tall baton. Next comes the color guard, then the drum line, beating out a loud cadence. I look eagerly down the rows of reed players, trumpets, and trombones, until I spot Will. We all hoot and cheer as he marches past, and I don't care how silly the uniforms are. Will looks totally handsome. I'm smiling and blushing at the same time.

But there isn't a moment to lose. As soon as Will passes, I throw my jeans around my neck as if they were a scarf and take off at a run.

"See you later, guys!" I call over my shoulder as I go. "Have fun at the Homecoming game!"

I manage to make my way through the parade crowd and onto the next block, which isn't so jammed up with people. As I'm sprinting down Dogwood Avenue, still hearing the sound of the drums, I feel lighter than air.

Not only did I get to *watch* the parade, which I wasn't expecting, I got to be in it — which I *really* wasn't expecting! I got to see Will in his marching band uniform, got to eat Jolly Cow ice cream (one bite does count), made friends with a whole bunch of cheerleaders, and surprised the pants off Kayleigh Carell. What an incredible day!

Then I turn onto Underhill Avenue and practically faint. There are four or five cars lined up behind the parade barricades, but the Cinderella Cleaners van, with its telltale crown on the roof, is no longer there.

Did Cat *leave*? Yes, I *have* been gone much longer than she would expect, but she wouldn't take off without at least calling me! Then I remember that I left my phone in my coat pocket, inside the van. So there's no way that she could have reached me. But she wouldn't drive back to the cleaners without me — Cat would never do that. She must be out looking for me, but where?

I think for a moment. Cat would have no way of knowing that I rode down Main Street on the cheerleaders' float, so she'd probably head toward the church parking lot, where I was supposed to be dropping off Marina's uniform and the Homecoming crowns. That makes sense, right?

I start down the block in that direction, but my legs feel a little bit shaky. What if she isn't there? How will I ever get back to the cleaners? And what in the world will I tell my *dad*?

But I don't have to answer those questions, thank goodness. As soon as I round the corner, I see the van parked on the side of the road. I breathe a huge sigh of relief. Cat flashes her headlights at me, and I run to the passenger door.

"Boy, am I glad to see *you*!" I say, getting into the seat. "We've got to hurry."

"Oh, really?" Cat says in sarcastic tones. "Why, do you think we're *late*?"

"Cat —" I start.

"Seat belt," she says, and I nod, pulling it over my shoulder as she starts the van. "Where have you been all this time?" she cries. "I've been climbing the walls!"

"You're not going to *believe* this," I say, but before I can tell her about being in the parade, she says three words that stop my heart cold.

"Your dad called."

"He did?" I gulp. "What did you tell him?"

We turn onto Underhill Avenue. Cat shoots me a look as she drives down the hill. "I *told* him that we'd gotten stuck in parade traffic, which was true. That you'd gotten out of the van to try to find out what was going on — which was also true, sort of — and that you'd be right back. Which I *thought* was true. But you've been gone for at least half an hour. Where were you?"

"Long story," I say, which must get the understatement

of the year prize. "But I did get the dress and the crowns to Marina. Was Dad really mad?"

"Why else would he call to check up on us?" Cat's voice is grim. "And that was at least fifteen minutes ago. If I lose my job over this . . ."

"You won't," I say quickly. "It's completely my fault. You were waiting for me. So if anyone's going to get fired, I'm the one."

I take a deep breath as I ponder this very real possibility. What would it be like if I *did* get fired? I stare out the window and try to imagine my life without Cinderella Cleaners. I would have more time on my hands. I'd be able to go to the *Snow Queen* rehearsals — not just during tech week, but for the whole show — and hang out with my friends.

But I wouldn't have Nelson. I wouldn't have Cat. And no way on earth would I *ever* have gotten to stand at the top of a cheerleading pyramid!

As soon as Cat and I get to the cleaners, we go straight to Dad's office. Cat has to give him the keys to the van, and if he's going to yell at us for being so late, I'd rather he do it in private. Joyless and Lara shoot us twin glares as we pass, but I don't make eye contact. Neither does Cat.

Dad looks up from his desk as we enter. He doesn't *seem* angry, but sometimes he gets very quiet and it's hard to tell.

"I'm so sorry, Mr. Donato," Cat says. "We got stuck in parade traffic coming and going. They had barricades up on Underhill Avenue."

"We'll both skip our lunch break, okay?" I add quietly.

"Sounds fair enough." Dad's voice is even. He looks at us both. "Was there anything else?"

Cat and I look at each other, confused by his lack of reaction. "Not really," I tell him, and Cat shakes her head.

"Good," he says. "Then you should get back to work."

"Can you believe it?" says Cat as we hang up our coats and get back in our smocks. "Your dad must have taken the world's largest chill pill."

"I think it's called Papa," I say. "I bet they had a father-son talk before Papa went home."

"Whatever. As long as it worked," says Cat, closing her locker. "Did I mention I totally love your grandfather? I hope I have half that much style when I'm his age."

"You will," I say, smiling. "You'll be a total gray fox." We head into the workroom and pick up right where we left off. It still seems too good to be true, but I'm not asking questions. I just hope Lara doesn't decide that we got off too easy and tell Dad about the elf costume. That "not yet" is haunting me.

As Cat and I work, I look up at the clock and mentally tick though Homecoming events. The Homecoming court ceremony takes place right after the parade. I wish I could be there to watch as Marina sets the crowns on the king's and queen's heads and everyone cheers. But there's no chance of that — it might even have happened already.

After the royals are crowned, there's a big town-wide picnic. The Chamber of Commerce grills hot dogs and hamburgers, local stores donate soda and chips, and LaToria's Bakery bakes giant Homecoming cakes, frosted in white with blue decorations. Even the local farm stand gets in on the act, donating bushels of late-season apples.

The picnic goes on until three, and then the football game starts. Cinderella Cleaners stays open till five on Saturdays, so by the time we get up to the high school athletic field, it'll be almost five-thirty. We'll probably catch the tail end of the game, but the part that I want to see most is the halftime show, and that's sure to be over and done with by then.

But I can't really complain about missing all the excitement today. As I'm rolling bins full of clothes back and forth, or hanging clean dresses on hangers with We Love Our Customers paper sleeves, I put the parade on a mental REWIND button, playing my favorite parts over and over. It makes the afternoon zoom past.

Still, I'm utterly shocked when Dad comes back into the workroom to tell me and Cat we can go.

It can't be closing time already, can it?

I look up at the clock and it's not even four. "I don't get it," I tell him.

Dad shrugs. "It's a slow afternoon, and I know you girls want to get up to the Homecoming game. You've been working hard ever since you got back. Take the last hour on me."

"Really?" says Cat, her eyes widening.

"Why not?" says Dad. For a moment, his face looks like Papa's. "You only live once, right?"

"You're the greatest!" I say, flying into his arms for a hug.

The high school parking lots are crammed to overflowing, and finding a place to park Cat's new car takes us a while. As we're getting out, we hear a loud drumroll, followed by trumpets.

"Quick," says Cat. "They must be starting the half-time show!"

We scurry across the parking lot toward the football field. I want to look for my friends, and I'm sure Cat is hoping to find Jared. But for now, we stand at the foot of the bleachers, where we have a really good view of the field.

In the center, a wide strip of grass has been spray-painted blue. Sitting high on two thronelike gold chairs are the Homecoming king and queen. I don't recognize the boy and girl, but I assume they're two popular seniors. The boy wears a royal blue tux and the girl a white satin prom dress. I look at the crowns on their heads and feel a surge of pride. They won't ever know it, but I made that happen. Without me, their heads would be bare.

The marching band and color guard are arranged in a giant half-circle behind the Homecoming thrones. At the drum major's signal, the band starts playing the high school's alma mater, "We Are Weehawken." The crowd in the stands sings along. So do we.

At the end of the song, the whole crowd starts sitting and standing in rhythm, raising their hands in a Wave pattern.

As the left side rises up with a roar, I spot my friends in the third row and wave to them, jumping up and down so I'll catch their eye. Jess waves back, looking almost as amazed to see me at the game as in the parade. She points to an empty spot on the bleachers right next to her.

"Let's go join them!" I say to Cat, but she's spotted a group of her own friends a bit farther up. We give each other a quick hug good-bye. Then I squeeze up the steps to sit down next to Jess, Ethan, Riley, Amelia, and Sara.

Meanwhile, the marching band splits into two rows, peeling off to both sides. The cheerleading squad runs down the center and launches into a high-energy halftime routine full of cartwheels, flips, and high-flying formations. I watch Marina and Becca flip through the air. This time it's my jaw that's dropping.

Ethan leans across Jess to tell me, "Good thing they replaced you for *this* part!"

"No kidding!" I can barely believe what my new friends are doing out there on that field. They're like gymnasts and dancers and acrobats rolled into one. Marina's especially energetic and limber. I can't take my eyes off her.

At least not until I remember that somebody else I know is performing. I look down the rows of band members marching in place and spot Will with his silver euphonium. I feel very proud of my sort-of-maybe boyfriend.

And that's when I realize someone is missing. I turn and ask Jess, "Hey, where is Jason?"

Ethan says, "He ditched her."

"He did *not*," says Jess, swatting his arm.

"He made plans with you and didn't show up," Ethan says. "I call that a ditch. Is there some other word for it in preppy-ese?"

Jess says, "Ethan, shut up." I can tell she's not kidding;

I hope he can, too. She turns back toward me to explain. "Jason was texting me all morning long. He forgot it was Parents Day at the Foreman Academy, and he had to go out to some stupid restaurant with his roommate's parents."

"What about *his* parents?" I ask.

"Jason hasn't seen them since August. He's really bummed out," Jess says with a sigh.

Three months. That's a really long time, even when you're at boarding school. "Is he going home for Thanksgiving, at least?" I ask.

She shakes her head. "They're flying him over for three days in Paris."

"I hate when that happens," moans Ethan. Jess shoots him an angry look and he quickly says, "Sorry."

Did Ethan the Sarcastic just *apologize*? That means he must care what Jess thinks. This is huge.

I lock eyes with Amelia, then Sara. Looks like they noticed, too.

I wonder, with all of the teasing Jess and Ethan do — could he actually *like* her? That would be hilarious.

Especially since he just broke up with Kayleigh, and seemed so interested in Marisol the other day.

Wow, I think, looking at Ethan. *You sure put the drama in Drama Club.*

But Jess is still totally focused on Jason, and I'm a good friend. I listen and nod as she talks about the Fourth Jonas and his fancy family vacations all over the world.

I still can't believe that I get to be here at the Homecoming game, surrounded by old friends and watching my new ones perform their amazing routine. It was so cool of Dad to let me and Cat take off early, and I'm really grateful.

There's a word for the way I feel right at this moment: *lucky*. I think about standing on top of that pyramid, stretching my arms to the sky, and I can't help but smile. I am one lucky girl.

Chapter Nine

That satisfied glow is still with me when I wake up on Sunday morning. After setting my alarm clock for school all week, and for work yesterday, it's a pleasure just to be able to laze around in my bed without hitting the snooze button. I lie on my back looking up at my attic room ceiling, which is covered with *Playbill*s from every show I've ever seen. The sunlight spills in through my bedroom window, and I can't help reviewing the glories of yesterday afternoon, flipping through the memories inside my head like a series of scenes from a movie. I still can't believe how cool all the cheerleaders turned out to be, and how much they all helped me.

All this, and I still get to be in *The Snow Queen*! I get into the shower and practice my song. The acoustics are great with the sound bouncing off the tiles. I hope I sound half as good in a real auditorium.

It doesn't feel as if anything could burst my bubble. Not my bratty stepsisters, who I can hear downstairs having their daily fight about who stole whose clothes. Not knowing I'll have to do all the breakfast prep chores so Fay can get her Sunday beauty rest. Not even French homework.

It's a short school week — Thanksgiving's on Thursday and we get Wednesday and Friday off, too, so only the most hard-core teachers are giving assignments for Monday and Tuesday. Madame Lefkowitz gave us a whole raft of worksheets with blanks to fill in. But as they say in France, so what?

I pull on my bathrobe and head downstairs. Dad's in the kitchen refilling his coffee.

"I wondered when you would get out of the shower," he says. "I almost went to the bakery without you."

"You wouldn't!" I tell him.

"Well, Papa and Nonni are coming, and I want to get everything ready so Nonni won't try to do all the work."

"Give me two minutes," I tell him, and charge back upstairs to get dressed. Every Sunday Dad and I drive to

LaToria's Bakery and bring back a box of fresh pastries for brunch, along with the Sunday *New York Times* and the local newspaper. Sometimes Dad also makes eggs or French toast, or whips up fruit smoothies or fresh-squeezed orange juice. It's my favorite meal of the week.

Of course, now that my grandmother's here, every meal will be a masterpiece.

Nonni's only been in New Jersey for thirty-six hours, and she's already done enough grocery shopping and cooking to feed a small army. It's a big treat for me and Dad — Nonni is a fabulous cook, and she makes the same recipes she taught Mom. Even the twins enjoyed her baked ziti and garlic bread last night, although Ashley turned green at the sight of the escarole soup.

Fay doesn't care much for cooking, but she doesn't enjoy someone else taking over her kitchen. She and Nonni are already starting to squabble about who's making what for Thanksgiving. My vote is that Nonni makes everything, but I'd never dare say so to Fay.

"How'd I do?" I gasp to Dad, skidding back into the kitchen in a purple fleece hoodie, pink T-shirt, and jeans.

"Two minutes flat," he says. "Very impressive."

LaToria's makes the best croissants around, and we get a dozen (six plain and six chocolate), a pecan swirl coffee cake (Papa's favorite), two cherry-cheese Danish, two jelly donuts, and two low-fat blueberry muffins.

"Something for everyone," Dad declares, adding a loaf of Italian bread and a sliced pumpernickel. It's a lot of baked goods, but whatever we don't eat today will be break-fast and school lunch tomorrow. We pick up the two Sunday papers and head for the car. The croissants in the bag are still warm, and I hug them against my chest.

"Who won the game?" Dad asks as we're driving back home. "I forgot to ask you at dinner last night."

"The Blue Jays!" I say. "We were awesome."

"What was the score?"

I try to remember. "Twenty-six to eighteen. Or it might have been twenty-eight to sixteen, I'm not totally sure."

"I'll check in the paper," says Dad. "Remember, I was a Blue Jay once, too."

Dad was on the track team in high school. He ran hurdles and still has his varsity jacket somewhere in the back of the closet.

"That was so nice of you, letting me and Cat get off early to go to the game," I tell him.

"It was nice of you rushing that uniform back to Cat's friend," he says. "That's how you make loyal customers, going that extra mile."

So it *was* Papa who convinced him. I've been hearing that "extra mile" line all my life. I make a mental note to thank Papa later.

"Cat's friends seemed like very sweet girls," Dad says.

"They were the bomb," I say fervently, and he looks back at me with raised eyebrows.

" 'The bomb' is a *good* thing? Like 'sick'?"

"Duh," I reply, and Dad lets out a sigh.

"Thirteen-year-olds should come with subtitles," he says, turning onto our street.

Fay and the girls are awake and dressed when we get back home, but of course they've left setting the table to me. I don't really mind, especially since I get to arrange the huge platter of pastries.

Fay looks at the mound of croissants and frowns. "Honestly, Frank. That's enough for a week!"

148

"It's a festive occasion," says Dad, pouring orange juice and raspberries into the blender. "Diana, can you give me one of those frozen bananas?"

I love Dad's fruit smoothie concoctions. As I take the ziplock bag out of the freezer, I hear our neighbors' two papillon dogs yapping up a storm, and look out the window. My grandparents have just pulled up in the little red-and-black Smart Car Papa rented. It looks like a ladybug, especially parked next to Fay's big white SUV.

"Look, it's the microcar!" Ashley says. The car was a huge hit with both twins last night, and they barrel outside for a closer look. Dad and I follow.

"Good morning, all!" says Papa. "Frank, you've got yourself some crop of beautiful girls." He gives me a kiss.

"I can't believe you found something even smaller than the Florida Orange," says Dad, shaking his head. In Miami Beach, Papa zips around town in a bright orange Mini Cooper.

"Next thing you know he'll have me on the back of a scooter," says Nonni, unfolding herself from the passenger seat. I go over to give her a hug, and she squeezes my hand, holding on to it tightly.

"I'm saving a fortune on gas," Papa shrugs. "What do I need, trunk space? And I can park on a dime."

"Can I have a ride after breakfast?" asks Brynna.

"Of course you can, Ashley."

"I'm Brynna," she pouts.

Papa squints at her. "No way. You're Ashley, she's Brynna. You can't kid a kidder."

"I'm Ashley, *she's* Brynna," says Ashley.

"You had the pink barrette yesterday, and now it's on *her* head?" says Papa. "You're doing this just to fool the old man."

"*She* had the pink barrette yesterday," Ashley says.

"He can do this for hours," I tell the twins, grinning. It's so good to see Papa and Nonni again.

We fill up on pastries and raspberry smoothies. Papa brews espresso in his special pot, and we get down to the serious business of sorting out newspaper sections. The twins want the funnies from the local paper. I go for the *New York Times* Arts & Leisure, with all the new movies and Broadway shows. Fay takes both Real Estate sections, plus the *Times* Style section so she can read about weddings. Papa stakes out the maga-zine, folding it open to the Sunday crossword, which he'll do with Nonni. Dad picks up the *Times* Week in Review and then, as an afterthought, reaches for the local sports section. I guess he wants to read about the Homecoming game.

I'm sitting right across from him. As he lifts the sports section and opens it up, I spot a big color photograph on the back page that floods me with horror.

It's the varsity cheerleaders on their parade float. They're in a pyramid, and right on the top is . . .

Me.

There I am, grinning my head off, my arms open wide in a perfect high V. And I'm wearing a customer's garment!

I flash back to the man with the tripod. How could I have been so stupid? I will be so, so busted if Dad sees that photo. And I bet I won't just lose my job at the cleaners. If he's really angry, which seems pretty likely, he might not let me be in the play either.

This is the end of my life as I know it.

I've got to do something. But what?

Dad is flipping through pages, looking for the Homecoming coverage. It's a matter of moments until he gets to the back page. I glance at the table between us. Splashing Dad's coffee is out of the question: too dangerous. But I still have a bit of my raspberry smoothie left. It's risky, but what are my options?

I pick up my glass and, with a loud inhaling sound, suck up the dregs through a straw. Then I lean forward, faking a sudden coughing fit as if I just swallowed wrong.

Splat! Pink liquid all over the photo!

"Ew, gross!" Ashley says as Brynna dissolves into giggles and Fay says, "Diana!" Just as I'd hoped, Dad drops his paper, coming over to thump me on the back as I splutter and cough.

"I'm okay," I gasp. "Sorry!" My fake cough was so violent I'm almost choking for real. Tears run down my cheeks, which I guess serves me right.

"Drink some water," says Papa.

I nod, grabbing the sports section as I rush to the kitchen sink, wheezing, "I'll get this cleaned up."

I have to admit, I'm impressed with my aim. In the photo, there's now a big splat of raspberry smoothie right over my face. It isn't too much of a stretch to scrub it so hard with a wet paper towel that the newsprint soaks through and gets torn. Whew!

I take a deep breath, splash my red face with cold water, then grab a wet sponge and go back to the table to clean up the spill. But Nonni has already wiped it all up with a napkin.

"Are you all right, honey?" she says, and I nod.

"I am so sorry," I tell everyone in a hoarse voice I don't have to fake. I really did make myself cough. Method acting, or just rotten luck?

Whatever, the crisis has passed. I dutifully clear off the rest of the glasses and plates from the table. Papa gets up to refill his espresso. As he's pouring it into the tiny white cup, he glances down at the soaked, shredded sports page I've left in the sunlight to dry off and reads Dad the headline.

"Twenty-six–eighteen, Blue Jays, in case you were wondering."

"Thank you!" says Dad.

Papa looks at the remains of the cheerleader photo. "First cherry slushie, then raspberry smoothie. That cheerleader suit is a magnet for trouble."

He has no idea how right he is.

Chapter Ten

On Monday, first thing in the morning, I run into Will in the hall by our lockers. It's great to see him back in his own clothes: a T-shirt from MGMT's latest tour and a pair of black jeans.

"Hi, Diana," he says, and I feel that little flutter of breathless excitement that lets me know we're something more than just friends, even if we don't have words for it yet. I'm determined to say something more than hi back, but the best I can muster is "How's it going?" Not too impressive.

"Good," says Will, and we look at each other. Have we already run out of things to say? He had the shy problem before we became kind-of sort-of whatever we are, but I didn't. Now every word feels too important, and like it'll come out all wrong.

"It was great to see you marching in the parade," I tell him.

Apparently that's the release he needed, because he breaks into one of his adorable Will Carson grins and says, "I hear you were in the parade yourself."

"It just sort of happened," I tell him, my cheeks turning pinker. "I had to bring someone a cheerleader outfit."

"And you wound up wearing it," Will says with a knowing smile. "Funny how often that happens to you."

"It must be an actress thing, I guess. The whole world's a costume shop. Speaking of which, I liked your band uniform."

"Well, that makes one of us," Will says.

"I thought it was . . ." I can't say *cute*. "Blue. It was very blue."

Both of us laugh. Then the bell rings, and after an embarrassed how-should-we-say-good-bye moment, we both mutter "Bye" at the same time and scurry in different directions for homeroom. I won't get to see Will again until lunch, and that feels like forever.

• • •

My first class after homeroom is gym, which is usually not my idea of how to start off Monday morning. But today promises to be better than usual. As I'm getting changed into my newly washed tank top and track shorts, Kayleigh comes by in her Hollister V-neck and Juicy Couture shorts.

"How did *you* get on that float?" she demands. "You're not a varsity cheerleader! Or a cheerleader at all!"

"Oh," I say airily, "I'm actually good friends with some of the girls from the high school cheerleading team."

Kayleigh looks stunned. *"What?"*

Amelia, whose gym locker is right across from mine, glances up and shrugs. "Hey, Diana's got connections. Her family knows everybody."

That's even sort of the truth, thanks to Cinderella Cleaners. I'm expecting Kayleigh to say something snooty, but her face goes suddenly wistful.

"Will you introduce me sometime?" she says in the smitten tones of a true fan. "Their preshow routine was just awesome!"

At last, something Kayleigh and I can agree on.

"They were incredible, weren't they?" I say, and she actually *smiles* at me.

"Buh-bye," she says cheerfully. "See you in the gym."

Maybe it won't be so bad being cast in *The Snow Queen* with Kayleigh Carrell. As I bend down to lace up my gym sneakers, I can feel a smile spreading across my face, and I can't help breathing a sigh of relief.

My sense of relief doesn't last very long. As soon as I get to the cleaners, I can tell something is wrong. I'm walking across the parking lot, where I'm happy to spot Papa's SmartCar, when I realize Lara is staring at me through the front window. That's nothing unusual — she's had it in for me ever since she got promoted. But the look on her face is the sheer, gloating triumph of someone who's finally got what she wanted.

Have I made up with Kayleigh just in time to get into more trouble with Lara? I quicken my pace as I walk around back to the employee entrance.

Everything seems pretty normal — the row of punched time cards, the coffee and soda machines, and the rack of green smocks. But I have the creepy sensation that some other shoe is about to drop. Probably right on my head.

My heart's beating fast as I hang up my backpack, pin my name tag onto my smock, and head into the workroom. Am I imagining things, or are Mr. and Mrs. Chen and Chris looking at me like I've done something wrong?

I wish Cat were here. But as always, it's taken her longer to drive all the way down from the high school than it took me on the middle school bus. I take a deep breath and push open the swinging doors into Customer Service. I'm so tense that when the conveyor belt I call the Dress Parade starts to move overhead, I nearly jump out of my skin. Lara is operating the foot pedal, and she gives me that same I've-got-you-now look.

MacInerny glances away from the customer she's been helping and tells me, "Your father wants to speak with you. Right away."

I gulp. All three of the customers standing in line look over at me, like they're wondering what kind of trouble I'm in.

They're not the only ones.

The door to Dad's office is shut, which must mean he's meeting with someone important. I give MacInerny a look, wondering if I should knock, but she just repeats, "Right away."

I knock on the door and hear Dad say, "Come in." I'm holding my breath as I swing the door open. Dad's sitting at his desk across from his accountant, Morris Smilow. Instead of giving me his usual warm smile, Dad turns to Morris and says, "Could you excuse us a minute?"

"Of course," Morris says. He sounds serious, too, and for a moment I think there must be some bad financial news Dad wants to share with me. What could have happened? And then I see Dad reach for something on top of his file cabinet.

It's the back page of the Sunday sports section. My heart turns to ice.

"Come with me, Diana," he says. I nod, feeling so nervous I'm practically paralyzed. I nearly trip over my feet as we go back out into the customer section. Dad smiles at a customer leaving with a plaid coat in a dry-cleaner bag.

"So long, Mrs. Pomerantz," he says, holding the door for her. "Thank you for coming."

"Thank *you*," she twinkles, charmed by his politeness.

But there are still two more customers waiting in line. Dad's not going to give me a lecture in front of *them*, is he? Not to mention Miss MacInerny and Lara.

But he takes me into the Tailoring section instead. My heart sinks as we go through the door. It might give us more privacy from customers, but it's chock-full of people I care about. Papa's standing at the cutting table, where he and Nelson are repairing a garment I recognize as the beaten-up trench coat Papa bought at Goodwill. Loretta and Sadie are both hard at work on their sewing machines. From the looks on their faces, I get the impression all four of them know what's coming.

Dad holds up the newspaper, and I see that the photo's been circled with the bright yellow chalk we use to mark garments that have stains or need tailoring.

"Can you explain this, Diana?" he says in the quiet voice he always uses when he's really upset.

I wince. Over Dad's shoulder I see Papa and Nelson looking at me sympathetically. That gives me courage.

"I had to deliver that uniform to Marina," I say.

"So you put it on?" Dad sounds skeptical.

"I had to." I start speaking quickly. "The coach wouldn't let me get through unless I was parade personnel. So I put on the uniform and tried again." I see Papa nod with what looks like approval, and tell Dad, "I thought I was going that extra mile."

"Go on," Dad says evenly.

"By the time I got to the cheerleaders' float, Marina was already hidden, and there wasn't time to trade clothes until later. So I . . . sort of rode in the parade."

"And did cheering routines," Dad says.

"Well, I tried. It was the only way," I say weakly.

Dad fixes me with a long look. Then he says, "What about yesterday morning at brunch, when you sprayed that raspberry smoothie all over my paper?"

"I was totally shocked," I say. "I saw that photo and spluttered at just the wrong moment."

"In the movies, they call it a spit-take," says Papa.

Dad turns toward him. "Pop, let me handle this, please." Papa raises both hands in apology. Dad turns to face me.

"So you're telling me it was an *accident* that you just happened to ruin this photo before I could see it?"

I hesitate. It wasn't really an accident, and it sounds like Dad already knows that. I might as well face the music and tell him the truth. "I might have scrubbed it with water a little too hard," I admit, glancing down. "I did sort of do that on purpose."

"Destroying the evidence," Papa says, stopping short when Dad shoots him a glare.

"Well . . . he's right," I admit to Dad. "I was so scared you'd be furious at me."

"I'm very upset," Dad says, still without raising his voice. "And disappointed by your lack of judgment. We've already been through this more than once, and I just don't see how you could have done —"

There's a knock on the door, and Lara comes in with a green garment draped over one arm. "I haff jacket for Tailorink," she says. "Is this a bad time?"

"I'm speaking with Diana," Dad tells her.

"Yes, I am seeink that. Maybe Diana can tell how this comes to be ripped." She holds up the green jacket. It's half of the elf suit I tried on last week, and under one arm is a torn seam, circled in the same bright yellow chalk as the newspaper.

Oh, she is evil!

"Diana?" says Dad. I can't speak.

"Last week I see her and Cat tryink these costumes on in the fur storage," Lara says.

"Why didn't you speak to me then?" Dad asks Lara.

"I don't like to say bad about people," says Lara.

Nelson clears his throat loudly in disbelief. "Um, excuse me," he says. I want to hug him.

Lara narrows her eyes at him, then turns back to Dad. "But when I see it has been torn like this . . ."

It was torn before, I want to scream at her, but who would believe me?

"Thank you, Lara," says Dad. He looks at me for a long time with an expression of such sadness I feel like I'm going to burst into tears on the spot. Then he speaks quietly. "Diana, I don't see how you can keep working here."

"What?" I gasp at the same moment as Papa and Nelson.

"It's hardly the first time we've had such an incident. You're already paying for gift certificates for two different customers. What am I supposed to do?" Dad asks. "I keep cutting you slack, and you keep on getting in trouble."

"I know," I say miserably. "But —"

"No buts," says Dad. "Employees do not borrow customers' clothes, ever. That is a cardinal rule."

I see Nelson shift uncomfortably, and I remember the time I caught him in a silk shirt he plucked off the Dress Parade. That was how we became friends.

But knowing that Nelson has borrowed clothes too doesn't make me feel any less guilty. How could I scheme and tell lies to my father, who's done so much for me, and who even let me and Cat stay for the Homecoming game on a busy workday? I hang my head, feeling about two feet tall. I must be the worst person on earth.

"I'm so sorry," I whisper.

"You know," Papa speaks up, "life is long. I remember an incident back in the old days when some young employee went out on a Saturday night, wearing something dropped off by a customer."

"Pop?" Dad says in a warning tone, but Papa keeps right on talking.

"Must be a couple of decades ago. Maybe Loretta could help jog my memory?"

"I certainly can," says Loretta. "It was a three-piece white disco suit."

Sadie shakes her head. "It was a red leather jacket, like the one in that Michael Jackson video. You know, that 'Thrilla.' Shoulder pads out to here." She holds a hand high off one shoulder.

"Different night," says Loretta. "First time was the white suit. You looked like that Johnny Travolta. So handsome."

She's looking at Dad, who's turned a strange color. Could she possibly mean what I think she means?

Nelson hoots. "*You* used to borrow clothes, Mr. D? That's outrageous!"

"It was ages ago," Dad protests. "I was a teenager!"

"I rest my case," Papa shrugs. "So is Diana."

I'm staring with wide eyes. "Dad? Did you really take customers' clothes from the cleaners?"

"Thanks a bunch, Pop," says Dad. He glances back at me, frowning. "All right, maybe a couple of times. But that doesn't make it okay."

"Did you punish him?" I ask Papa.

"Of course. And he grew up good. Just like you will." He turns toward Lara, frowning. "You, I'm not so sure about."

It's official, world: Papa is my hero! It's worth any punishment Dad might come up with to see the expression on Lara's face.

Dad is looking at mine. "All right," he says after a beat. "You can keep your job here. But you owe me another four Saturdays after the holidays."

I nod. Is that all? It doesn't seem harsh at all — in fact, if Cat's still working weekends, it might even be fun.

But Dad isn't finished. "And I think I'll move you up front after Christmas, so Lara and Joy can keep an eye on you."

Gulp. That is *not* what I had in mind. Not at all. But the good news is, I wasn't fired. I'm still working at Cinderella Cleaners, and getting to be in *The Snow Queen*, so life is just fine.

Tuesday night marks the official beginning of Thanksgiving vacation, and Papa and Nonni invite Jess and me to come to their hotel for a swim in the heated pool. It's inside a big sun-roofed courtyard with palm trees and flowers. After our third or fourth dip in the pool and Jacuzzi, we're starting to feel like pickles, so we wrap up in white terry-cloth robes and lie side by side on two lounge chairs. Papa treats us both to Shirley Temples, and we feel like royalty, sipping our drinks by the pool.

"So have you heard from Jason in Paris?" I ask her, feeling very jet-set.

"He texted me once from the airport, but that was all. I was hoping to hear all about what they're doing, you know? He said he'd send pictures of the Eiffel Tower and his favorite crêpe stand. I wanted to see whipped cream crêpes."

"The overseas cell phone charges must be killer," I say sympathetically.

"That shouldn't be an issue. His family is filthy rich." Jess sounds more than a bit disappointed, so I change the subject.

"Are you looking forward to Thanksgiving dinner?" I ask.

"I guess," she says, sipping her drink. "Mom won this round, so it's just her and me and Dash. Oh, and my uncle might come from the city. But we probably won't even make a whole turkey."

"No stuffing?" I'm horrified. Stuffing, for me, is the main event.

"Maybe some Stove Top. My dad's family does the whole huge dinner thing with skazillions of cousins, but I didn't want Mom to be all by herself, so I didn't push. We'll go up to Connecticut and stay with my dad over Christmas, I guess." Jess takes a bite of her maraschino cherry. "I *love* these things. Too bad they're toxic."

I try to imagine what it would be like to have parents who don't get along with each other and live in two different states. It sounds really tough. Not that it's always a piece of cake living with Fay and my stepsisters.

I look over at Papa and Nonni, happily doing a crossword puzzle together poolside. How do they get along with each other so well, when nobody else seems to? It must just be practice.

• • •

Getting along well with Fay is a different matter. Nonni insists that the Thanksgiving meal should include homemade lasagna; Fay wants to make her candied yam casserole. They stare at each other across the stove.

"The Pilgrims did not serve lasagna at Plymouth Rock," Fay says. "It's not the tradition."

"Well, it's *our* tradition," says Papa, and I feel like cheering. My Nonni's lasagna is the best in the world. And who says the Pilgrims served marshmallow yams?

They finally agree to make both, since the twins will complain if there aren't candied yams.

"Yams and lasagna and stuffing is too many carbs," Fay grumbles. "Not to mention the pumpkin pie."

Nonni just shrugs. "That's what makes it a feast. You'll have plenty of leftovers after we leave." I hate to think of them flying back home to Miami Beach, but the week's almost over.

The first day of vacation is always delicious. There's something especially great about not waking up to an alarm clock on Wednesday morning. Papa and Nonni stop by our house shortly after Fay goes to her office. I come out to greet them as Papa circles around to help Nonni out of the passenger seat of the red microcar.

"Hello, darling Diana," she says, giving me a big hug.

Papa lifts up the hatch and starts unloading groceries. It looks like one of those circus routines where a whole troupe of clowns piles out of a tiny car. First comes a bushel of Roma tomatoes and several bunches of basil from our favorite farm stand. Next come two grocery bags from ShopRite, and a hand-cranked pasta machine that Nonni must have carried from Florida in her luggage.

"Are we going to make our own noodles?" I ask her, excited.

"Of course," Nonni says.

"No shortcuts for this one," says Papa.

"You can taste the difference," Nonni says. "Don't tell me it's not worth it."

"It's worth it, it's worth it," he says. "Every minute it takes."

I help Papa carry the groceries inside as Nonni walks up the path with her distinctive side-to-side wobble. Her legs are sturdy but a bit bowed, and I smile as I realize that she's replaced the heavy black shoes she always used to wear with Velcro sneakers in Miami pastels.

Once we're inside, Papa gives Nonni a kiss on top of her head, ruffles my hair, and takes off to meet Dad at the cleaners. Fay is at work, and Ashley and Brynna are sleeping late on their first day of vacation, so I've got Nonni all to myself. We unload the groceries onto the kitchen counter. There's ricotta and fresh mozzarella, olive oil, garlic, sweet onions, and sausage. There's also semolina flour, cornmeal, and eggs.

"Is that for the pasta?" I ask.

"Yes, and we're going to bake cornbread for tomorrow's stuffing."

Hooray! I can't wait to make that!

"But first," Nonni says, "I'm going to teach you my red sauce. Roll up your sleeves."

As we're working side by side, peeling garlic and dicing tomatoes, I can't help but picture my mother, smiling at me from this same kitchen counter. She would be so happy that Nonni is teaching me her cooking secrets. It almost feels like she's here with us. I wish her family — my other grandparents — lived closer to us, but they're in Seattle, where Mom grew up.

I think about all of the different families I know: Jess's divorced parents living in two different states; Jason's still-married but long-distance parents, who he rarely sees; Will's super-cool single dad; Amelia's mismatched ballerina mom and jock dad with one daughter who takes after each parent; Sara's giant extended family, who are planning to roast spicy turkey legs in the restaurant's tandoori oven. Everyone's got some good and some bad in the mix. The trick is the way things combine — just like making a stuffing.

The smells in the kitchen are so delicious on Thanksgiving Day that I feel like I'm going to go crazy from hunger. Ashley and Brynna make place cards for everyone, with pictures of pumpkins and apples and Indian corn. Mine has a picture of a turkey, which I decide not to take personally. It's just nine-year-old humor.

At long last, the feast is spread out on the table. Nonni's lasagna sits on a trivet next to the marshmallow-topped yam casserole, with side dishes of green beans and onions and cranberry sauce. Best of all is that huge bowl of cornbread stuffing, letting off fragrant steam right in front of my nose. I breathe in deeply and sigh.

Papa stands at the head of the table, ready to carve the first slices of turkey. But first he lifts up his glass full of cider, proposing a toast. "Here's to every last one of us," he says. "And here's to Cinderella Cleaners, and to my son and granddaughter, keeping it all in the family." He raises his glass to me, and my chest swells with pride.

We all clink glasses and drink. Then Fay says, "Why don't we go around the table and say what we're most thankful for?"

Ugh. Why don't we not? Is this from some after-school special Fay watched? The twins roll their eyes, and for once I agree with them.

But Fay doesn't notice that we're all annoyed (not to mention incredibly hungry!). She looks at Dad. "Frank, you go first."

Dad gets to his feet. "I'm thankful for you," he says simply, looking at each one of us. "For all of you, here at this table. For being together. And thanks, Mama, for your lasagna."

Nonni beams. Fay does not. She prompts, "Ashley?"

"Do I have to?" says Ashley.

"Tell us something you're thankful for," Fay says.

Ashley sighs and stands, rolling her eyes. "I'm thankful for Justin Bieber."

Brynna says, "Not fair! He was *mine*!"

"Well, I got him first," Ashley says. "Deal with it."

Brynna stands up. "*I'm* thankful for Justin Bieber. More thankful than her. And for Mommy's yams. Now can we eat?"

"In a minute, princess," Papa says with a twinkle. "Diana is next." He gestures that I should stand up, and I do.

Thank-you speeches are right up my alley. For years I've been watching the Oscars and the Tony awards, and I always imagine the gown I'd be wearing and what I would say as I clutch my statuette. I'd thank all the other nominees, because I think that's gracious. And all of the people I worked with — not just the cast and director, but all the designers and crew people, dressers and drivers and gaffers and grips. And then I'd thank the audience. Without people watching, there isn't a show.

But what am I *thankful* for? There's so much.

"I'm thankful for getting to be in *The Snow Queen*. I'm thankful I still have my wonderful job. I'm thankful for all my good friends. And" — I hesitate, just for a second — "even though Dad and Papa have already said it, I'm thankful for *us*. For my family."

"*Bravissima!*" Papa says, clapping. He looks over at Nonni.

She gets to her feet with a bit of an effort, raises her glass, and says in Italian, "*Grazie a tutta la famiglia.*" This means "thanks to the whole family," and hearing Nonni say it makes my eyes well up a little. "And *grazie* — thanks," she adds, "for this beautiful feast."

Papa claps again, and we all look at Fay. This was all her idea, but I can't imagine what Fay would be thankful for. Her SUV? Selling real estate? She'll probably say Ashley and Brynna, I think, sitting back in my chair with my arms folded.

Fay stands up. She's wearing her pastel peach pantsuit and gold button earrings, and with her stiff frosted hair, she looks like the host of an infomercial. She looks at each of us in turn. "I'm thankful to be in a family where there's so much love," she says, and there's a catch in her voice that I've never heard before as she looks at Dad. "I'll always be thankful for meeting you, Frank. Always, always." She turns toward Ashley and Brynna.

Here it comes, I think. Then I hear Fay say, "And I'm thankful for our three beautiful daughters."

Three? Did she just include *me*? Now *that* is a real surprise. That's actually *sweet*. I sit up a bit straighter.

"Hear, hear," Papa says. "To family. Let's eat."

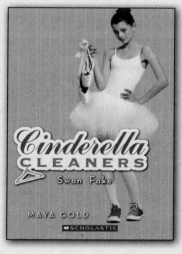

Ask her," says Sara, nudging Amelia's arm.

"Ask me what?" I say, trying not to drip cranberry sauce on my napkin.

Amelia sets down her fork. "It's a really big favor."

She's got my attention. I swallow. "What is it?"

Amelia sighs. "You know how I got myself roped into doing the *Nutcracker*?"

I nod, waiting for more.

"Well, the only reason I did it was so Mom would let me go to this incredible winter break soccer intensive with Sara."

"I did it last year," Sara says. "It was sick."

Amelia goes on. "So it turns out the tryouts are two weeks from Saturday, from noon to two." I nod again. Where is she heading with this? "That's the same afternoon as the *Nutcracker*'s matinee. Also at two."

"Oh, you're kidding," I say sympathetically. "That totally bites."

"Could you do it for me?" says Amelia.

For a moment I don't even know what she's asking. Do what? Then it dawns on me. "You want me to *dance ballet*?"

This is totally out of the question. I went to ballet school for maybe a year, when I was about six years old. After the first recital (the one where I tripped on my slipper), I switched over to tap and never looked back.

Besides, Amelia said two weeks from Saturday. So there's *really* no way. "That's opening night of *The Snow Queen*!" I tell her.

"At seven o'clock," says Amelia. "This is at two. You'd have plenty of downtime in between. Plus there's nobody else I can ask. I'm desperate."

This is a tough one. Amelia stuck her neck out to help me sneak into the Hunger Unmasked Halloween ball, and I really owe her a favor. But dancing *ballet*? When I have an opening night just a few hours later?

"I don't know, Amelia," I tell her. "I'd love to help out, but ballet isn't something you fake."

"Of course it is," says Amelia. "When I was little, I used to call the ballet *Swan Lake Swan Fake*. My mom would go, '*Lake*. It's *Swan Lake*!' But I was faking it then, and I'm faking it now, trust me."

"What are you playing again? A toy?"

Amelia nods. "A mechanical doll. I'll be back in time

for Act Two, when I have to actually dance. But I need you for the opening scene, where they take me out of a gift box and wind me up. I walk a few steps and slow down to a stop." She makes a robot movement, then freezes, head cocked to one side. "Piece of cake."

That does sound like something I could swan-fake, if it weren't for *The Snow Queen* being right afterward. I try a new tack. "But I don't look anything like you."

"Diana, I'm playing a *doll*. My face will be painted, I'm wearing a wig, and I move like a wind-up toy. No one would know you're not me."

"Not even your mom?" I ask.

Amelia just snorts. "She won't pay any attention to *me* — Zee is dancing the lead."

I'm running out of excuses. "But doesn't your mom know these soccer tryouts are on the same day?"

"We've already had seventeen fights about it," Amelia explains. "No way would I have agreed to *The Nutcracker* if I knew it meant missing the soccer trials, but now that I'm in it, Mom tells me I've 'made a commitment'" — Amelia makes air quotes with her fingers — "and the show must go on."

"She's right," I say. "Imagine if you didn't show up for a soccer game. It would totally stink for the rest of the team."

Will nods. He's been listening to this whole exchange, and I know he's imagining what it would do to a band if the bass player didn't show up for a gig.

Amelia agrees. "No, I get it, I know. I just want to do *both*. And I can. Just not before two o'clock. I have Mom's permission to go in the morning with Sara. I just had to swear up and down that I'll be back on time, in my costume and makeup, by half-hour call. This is where you come in."

Costume and makeup? It actually does sound appealing, except for the time crunch.

I hesitate, looking at Will. I have to admit that I like the idea of saving the day for Amelia.

"Can I let you know by the end of the school day?" I ask her.

CaNDY APPLe BooKS
Read them aLL!

Drama Queen

I've Got a Secret

Confessions of a Bitter
Secret Santa

Super Sweet 13

The Boy Next Door

The Sister Switch

Snowfall Surprise

Rumor Has It

The Sweetheart Deal

The Accidental
Cheerleader

The Babysitting Wars

Star-Crossed

Accidentally
Fabulous

Accidentally
Famous

Accidentally
Fooled

Accidentally
Friends

How to Be a Girly Girl in
Just Ten Days

Miss Popularity

Miss Popularity
Goes Camping

Making Waves

Juicy Gossip

Life, Starring Me!

Callie for President

Totally Crushed

Wish You Were Here,
Liza

See You Soon,
Samantha

Miss You, Mina

Winner Takes All